Fighting Franco's Fire

Out of the corner of his eye, Clint saw Jim Boone and his shotgun move onto the boardwalk. There was no flash of silver on his chest.

"Your call," he said to Franco.

Franco nodded, but before the nod was complete, his hand went for his gun. This was the signal for the others to draw as well.

Clint drew his gun and fired before anyone else. His first shot took Franco in the chest, drove him back a few feet. The shotgun blast shredded Rufus Holmes before the big man knew what had hit him.

DON'T MISS THESE
ALL-ACTION WESTERN SERIES
FROM THE BERKLEY PUBLISHING GROUP

THE GUNSMITH by J. R. Roberts
Clint Adams was a legend among lawmen, outlaws, and ladies. They called him . . . the Gunsmith.

LONGARM by Tabor Evans
The popular long-running series about Deputy U.S. Marshal Custis Long—his life, his loves, his fight for justice.

SLOCUM by Jake Logan
Today's longest-running action Western. John Slocum rides a deadly trail of hot blood and cold steel.

BUSHWHACKERS by B. J. Lanagan
An action-packed series by the creators of Longarm! The rousing adventures of the most brutal gang of cutthroats ever assembled—Quantrill's Raiders.

DIAMONDBACK by Guy Brewer
Dex Yancey is Diamondback, a Southern gentleman turned con man when his brother cheats him out of the family fortune. Ladies love him. Gamblers hate him. But nobody pulls one over on Dex . . .

WILDGUN by Jack Hanson
The blazing adventures of mountain man Will Barlow—from the creators of Longarm!

TEXAS TRACKER by Tom Calhoun
J.T. Law: the most relentless—and dangerous—manhunter in all Texas. Where sheriffs and posses fail, he's the best man to bring in the most vicious outlaws—for a price.

THE GUNSMITH

339

THE LADY DOCTOR'S ALIBI

J. R. ROBERTS

JOVE BOOKS, NEW YORK

THE BERKLEY PUBLISHING GROUP
Published by the Penguin Group
Penguin Group (USA) Inc.
375 Hudson Street, New York, New York 10014, USA

Penguin Group (Canada), 90 Eglinton Avenue East, Suite 700, Toronto, Ontario M4P 2Y3, Canada
(a division of Pearson Penguin Canada Inc.)
Penguin Books Ltd., 80 Strand, London WC2R 0RL, England
Penguin Group Ireland, 25 St. Stephen's Green, Dublin 2, Ireland (a division of Penguin Books Ltd.)
Penguin Group (Australia), 250 Camberwell Road, Camberwell, Victoria 3124, Australia
(a division of Pearson Australia Group Pty. Ltd.)
Penguin Books India Pvt. Ltd., 11 Community Centre, Panchsheel Park, New Delhi—110 017, India
Penguin Group (NZ), 67 Apollo Drive, Rosedale, North Shore 0632, New Zealand
(a division of Pearson New Zealand Ltd.)
Penguin Books (South Africa) (Pty.) Ltd., 24 Sturdee Avenue, Rosebank, Johannesburg 2196,
South Africa

Penguin Books Ltd., Registered Offices: 80 Strand, London WC2R 0RL, England

This is a work of fiction. Names, characters, places, and incidents either are the product of the author's imagination or are used fictitiously, and any resemblance to actual persons, living or dead, business establishments, events, or locales is entirely coincidental.

THE LADY DOCTOR'S ALIBI

A Jove Book / published by arrangement with the author

PRINTING HISTORY
Jove edition / March 2010

Copyright © 2010 by Robert J. Randisi.
Cover illustration by Sergio Giovine.

ISBN: 978-0-515-14765-0

JOVE®
Jove Books are published by The Berkley Publishing Group,
a division of Penguin Group (USA) Inc.,
375 Hudson Street, New York, New York 10014.
JOVE® is a registered trademark of Penguin Group (USA) Inc.
The "J" design is a trademark of Penguin Group (USA) Inc.

PRINTED IN THE UNITED STATES OF AMERICA

10 9 8 7 6 5 4 3 2 1

ONE

When Clint Adams rode into Veracruz, it was between French and United States possession. It had last been held by the French in 1861. Currently, they were ruling themselves. Porfirio Díaz had regained the presidency he'd held for a brief month, then taken back from Juan N. Méndez after three months. The Mexican people didn't know at the time—and neither did Díaz—that he would now hold that office until 1911.

Veracruz was a port town off the Gulf of Mexico, which was what made it so desirable as a possession. At the moment, it was desirable to Clint just as a place to get away for a while.

He directed Eclipse down the street, keeping his eye out for a livery stable. He didn't find one until he was within sight of the docks. He was about to turn around when he saw it and shrugged. It was as good a place as any, and there was a hotel right across the street. Neither would offer top-rated services, but Clint wasn't looking for the kind of amenities he usually liked. A room with a bed would do for him.

He dismounted in front of the livery, which, despite the fact that it was run-down, was clean—as barns go, that is. Favoring his left foot, he approached the front doors.

A man came out wiping his hands on his thighs, then stopped when he saw Eclipse. He stared at the Darley Arabian with wide eyes.

"Señor," he said, "that is the finest-lookin' animal I have ever seen."

Clint studied the man. Late fifties, rawboned with big jug ears. His hands were scarred, a sure sign of a man who had dealt with livestock most of his life. You can't handle horses for a living without having a finger or two bitten off.

"Can you care for him the way he should be cared for?" Clint asked.

"Señor, horses are my business," the man said. "I have never seed one like this before, but I know I will take the best care of him."

Clint held the reins out to the man.

"Then do it. I'll be staying in the hotel across the street."

"That is not such a nice place to stay, señor," the man warned him.

"That's okay," Clint said. "I'm not looking for such a nice place."

Clint turned, winced when he put his weight on his foot.

"Did you hurt your foot, señor?" the man asked.

"Twisted it," Clint said. "Is there a doctor around?"

"Sort of."

"What do you mean 'sort of'?"

"You will see," the man said. "The doctor's name is Doc Sugarman."

"Sugarman?"

"Sí, señor. When you check into the hotel, ask at the desk and they will direct you to the doctor's office."

"Thank you," Clint said.

"De nada, señor," the man said. "It is my honor to care for your horse."

"How much?" Clint asked.

"We do not need to speak of that now, señor. Another time."

"What's your name?"

"Ignacio."

"Gracias, Ignacio."

"Enjoy your stay, señor."

As Ignacio walked Eclipse into the stable, Clint crossed the street and entered the hotel.

The disinterested desk clerk allowed him to sign in and gave him a key.

"Gringo?" the lazy man asked.

"Yes."

"Top of the eh-stairs," the man said.

"Gracias."

Clint started for the stairs, then remembered he wanted to ask directions to the doctor, but since the clerk apparently didn't speak much English, he decided to wait. Maybe when he came down later there'd be someone else around who did speak English.

He got to his room, found the door unlocked. He entered, made sure the lock on the door worked by using the key, then closed it and locked it. The room looked neat, and although dusty, it wasn't what he would call dirty.

He dropped his saddlebags onto the bed, set his rifle down in a corner, then went to the window. The room overlooked the main street, but there was no access to his window from outside. Anybody wanting to get into his room by the window would have to walk up the side of the building.

He sat down on the bed and felt his foot. He didn't want to take the boot off because his ankle was swollen. He might not get the boot back on. He had to go see the doctor, just in case it was broken—although he didn't know what even a doctor could do. He'd never had a broken foot or ankle before.

There was water in a pitcher on the dresser, next to a basin. He poured some and washed his face and hands. It was brackish, but wet. Once he felt cleaner, he left the room and went back downstairs. The desk clerk was still the only one there. He had his elbow on the desk, his head in his hand, dozing.

"Excuse me," he said.

"Señor?"

"The doctor?" Clint asked. "Can you direct me to the doctor?"

"Sí, el médico," the clerk said. "Eh-outside, that way"— the man pointed to his left—"eh-two block."

"Two blocks?" Clint held up two fingers. "Dos?"

"Sí, dos," the man said, holding up two fingers. "Up eh-stairs."

"Two blocks that way, and upstairs."

"Sí."

"Gracias."

The man waved him off, went back to his nap. Clint left, hoping the directions were right.

TWO

Clint found the doctor's office right where the clerk said it would be. He would never have found it without the directions, because it wasn't marked at all. He saw a stairway and a door above a leather store, walked up, and knocked. A woman in a cotton dress, with a full figure, blond hair, and striking blue eyes, answered.

"Yes?"

"I'm sorry," he said. "I was told— I mean, I'm looking for a doctor named Sugarman?"

"You've come to the right place," she said, stepping back. "Come in."

He limped in past her, and it was probably the last steps he would have been able to take that day without a doctor. The foot was throbbing and he sank down thankfully into a chair.

"What happened to you?" she asked.

"I twisted it," he said. "Stepped into a chuckhole, like a tenderfoot."

"That could happen to anyone," she said. "Let's see if we can get that boot off without cutting it."

"Shouldn't we wait for the doctor?"

She crouched down in front of him, bent to the task, and said, "I am the doctor."

"Doc Sugarman?" he asked.

She looked up at him.

"That's right. Lissa Sugarman."

"Lisa?"

"Lissa," she said. "Two *s*'s." She sat back on her haunches and asked, "Still want me to look at your foot?"

"Well . . . sure," he said. "After all, you are the doctor."

"Well, lots of folks around here don't think so," she said.

"Because you're a woman?"

"A woman," she said, "and the blond hair, I think. Especially the Mexican men. They think a blond gringa is only good for one thing."

She looked back down at his foot, took it into her hands.

"Why do you stay, then?" he asked.

"I came down here to help these people," she said, "and that's what I intend to do."

"Well," he said, "I hope you'll help me before you start in on the whole city."

"Don't worry," she said. "I'm a long way from caring for this whole city." She gripped the boot firmly with both hands. "I think this'll come off."

He hoped she was talking about the boot.

The boot came off, but wouldn't go back on—not easily anyway.

"It's not broken, but you twisted it pretty good," Lissa Sugarman said.

She wrapped it, told him to try to stay off it for a few days.

"That won't be easy," he said. "I have to get around."

"Are you staying in Veracruz for a while?"

"I suppose," he said, "until my foot heals."

They struggled with the boot, trying to get it back on without hurting him. In the end he gritted his teeth and yanked it on. It fit snugly over the wrap.

"Actually, that's a good thing," she said. "It'll keep it immobile. How much walking do you intend to do?"

"I'm staying in a hotel," he said. "Up the stairs, I have to eat . . ."

"You can't just stay in your room?"

"I'm not staying in a very good hotel," he said. "In fact, it's just up the street, across from a livery stable."

"That place?" she asked.

"It's not that I can't afford a better place," he said. "I, uh, don't want to. I just want a place to sleep."

"I wasn't judging," she said.

"Yeah, you were."

She waved her hands. "Look where I am," she said. "Who am I to judge?"

"I get the feeling you could practice medicine in a lot of other places."

"Yes," she said, "all of them in the East, where I don't want to be."

"And North of the border?"

"Someday," she said. "Not yet."

Clint studied her. She appeared to be in her thirties.

"Thirty-eight," she said. "Practicing medicine for about twelve years. Came here a year ago."

"From where?"

"That's all the information you get," she said. "After all, I told you my age."

He stood, tested his foot by putting weight on it.

"How is it?"

"Better," he said. "I think I can walk back to the hotel."

"Walk slowly," she said, "and then stay there, at least until you need to eat."

"Everybody needs to eat, right?" he asked. "Even you?"

"I was just about to hand you my bill," she said. "Are you asking me to supper?"

"Well," he said, "I don't really know where to eat, do I? I could walk for miles before I find a place, do irreparable damage—"

"When you told me your name, it was familiar," she said. "It took me a while, but . . . are you the Gunsmith?"

"Does that make a difference?"

"I'd just like to know."

"Yes, I am."

"Are you down here hiding?"

"No," he said, "at least, not in the way you mean. No one's after me, I just wanted to take some time . . . away."

"I see."

"Supper?"

"Only if I can pick you up at your hotel with a buggy," she said. "I don't want you undoing the work I did."

"Deal."

THREE

Clint's foot was sore by the time he got back to his hotel, but he was going to be picked up by Doc Sugarman in a few hours, so he had that long to rest. He debated whether or not to take the boot off, decided to go ahead.

Lissa Sugarman had soaked his foot before treating it, gave him some extra bandages to take back to the hotel with him. She told him he could soak the foot in his room, and then rewrap it himself. It didn't have to be artful, just tight. He told her he'd had some experience with bandages before.

He relaxed in his room, soaking the foot, then rewrapping it. He stayed off it until it was time for him to meet the doctor out front. He struggled to pull his boot back on, then made his way down the stairs to the front door. As he came outside, Lissa pulled up in a buggy, all smiles.

"You're prompt," she said as he climbed into the buggy. "I like that in a man."

"I aim to please, ma'am."

She tossed a kiss at her horse and shook the reins.

"How's your foot?" she asked.

"Much better."

"Did you stay off it?"

"I did, and I soaked it and rewrapped it."

"You're a good patient."

"Where are we going to eat?"

"Better part of town," she said. "One of my favorite restaurants."

"They know you there?"

"I go a few times a month," she said. It wasn't really an answer.

He watched as the conditions of the street and the buildings improved in stages the farther they got from the docks.

"Why set up shop near the docks?" he asked. "Wouldn't you be more accepted in this area?"

"Maybe," she said, "but I wanted to go where I was needed."

"Only they don't know they need you, huh?"

"Not yet," she said, "but they're coming around. I'm actually getting some business right from the docks—sailors, teamsters, they need medical help quickly."

"And you're the nearest sawbones, huh?"

"Exactly."

Lissa Sugarman was not only a good doctor, she was a smart lady.

She pulled her buggy to a stop in front of a restaurant with two large plate glass windows. Etched on both windows was the name DOMINO'S. Clint thought the fancy lettering almost made it look as if it said DELMONICO'S—a famous New York steak house. He wondered if that was deliberate.

As they entered, a portly, middle-aged tuxedoed man came rushing over to them with a big smile on his face, and Clint knew the smile was not for him. Looking around the place, Clint wished he had dressed better.

"Ah, Doc Veracruz, so nice to see you again," the man said.

"Hello, Roscoe. Table for two?"

"For you? Of course. This way."

Lissa took Clint's arm. She was wearing a pretty red dress that didn't look expensive, but was certainly presentable. It was also tight enough to show off all her attributes. Men watched her walk across the floor, which made Clint proud that she was on his arm. Also, if they were looking at her, they weren't looking at him, which suited him.

The man showed them to a table, but Clint could see another table against the back wall, which he preferred.

"Could we get that one?" he asked, pointing.

"Of course, sir." He had dropped two menus onto the table, so now he picked them up and showed them to the other table.

"Ben will be your waiter," he told them.

"Thank you, Roscoe," Lissa said.

"Did I offend him asking for this table?" Clint asked. He didn't really care. He preferred to sit with a wall near him.

"I don't think so," she said. "He just didn't consider this one of his better tables. He was trying to please me."

"I don't want to damage your reception here in the future."

"Don't worry," she said. "I think Roscoe has a little crush on me."

"I think so, too."

FOUR

Clint could see why Domino's was Lissa's favorite restaurant. The steaks were perfectly prepared and the coffee was hot and strong.

"That name," Clint said when they had gotten to their desserts.

"What name is that?"

"'Doc Veracruz,'" Clint said. "Isn't that what he called you when we came in?"

She smiled.

"That's just something he calls me," she said. "A nickname."

"Does anybody else call you that, or just him?" Clint asked.

"It might be catching on," she said. "I'm finally starting to build up a list of patients."

"It must have been frustrating to you when you first arrived," he said. "I mean, not being accepted."

"It was extremely frustrating," she agreed. "Luckily, I

came here with some savings that I was able to live on until I started getting some patients."

"So you're able to make a living now?" he asked.

"No," she said. "I'm still not making enough money. I only have a few patients per week. Sometimes, when a ship comes in, there'll be a rush. Deckhands usually arrive with some kind of injury, or ailment. That's when it helps that I'm the closest physician."

"Why don't you have a shingle out?"

"I did have," she said. "Someone took it down the first day. I replaced it, but it was removed again. After a few more times I finally stopped."

"So then how do they find you?"

"The word gets around," she said. "How did you find me?"

"I see your point."

"I went around and talked to several of the hotels in the area. In exchange for free treatment for their employees, they agreed to send me business."

"That was a smart move," he said. "So, where in the East did you come here from?"

"I sort of worked my way here," she said. "I spent some time in Saint Louis and Kansas City, a little bit in Texas, before I finally settled in Veracruz."

He noticed she hadn't answered the question about where she had started from. He decided if she didn't want to talk about it, he wouldn't push her.

On the other side of the restaurant a man and woman tried not to stare at Dr. Sugarman and the man she was with.

"There's that woman," the lady said. "She hasn't left town yet?"

Her husband stole a look over his shoulder, then back across the table at his wife.

"Don't worry, Lillian," he said. "It's being handled."

"By who?" she demanded. "Not by you, that's for sure. When will you be a man and do something, Oliver?"

Oliver Graham stared at his wife, wishing he were man enough to put a bullet into her face—or at least his fist. He knew men who kept their women in line by hitting them, but they had apparently started very early. Graham had already been married to Lillian for twenty years, and in all that time had never laid a hand on her in anger. His friend, Henry Colter, had once told him he should have smacked Lillian the first night of their honeymoon, just to make the point that he was in charge. Oliver had never told Henry they didn't even have a honeymoon.

"Lillian . . ."

"What, Oliver?" she demanded. "What? Are you going to warn me about something?" She drew out the word *waaaarn* to mock him. "That woman is going to start cutting into your business, you mark my words. It wouldn't surprise me if she was a doctor *and* a whore. How would you compete with that?"

Certainly not with you turning tricks, he wanted to tell her. No man would pay for her wrinkled face and breasts.

"It's being handled, Lillian," he said, "so stop throwing hateful glances over that way."

"Hateful?" she demanded. "You think I'm hateful?"

He knew his wife hated Lissa Sugarman more for

being beautiful than for being a doctor, but if he said so, he'd never hear the end of it. Maybe he should say it, though. By the time they got home, he might be ready to go ahead and put that bullet in her face.

"What are you going to do, Oliver?" she demanded.

"I'm going to have a slice of apple pie, my dear," he said.

FIVE

"Do you know the couple who is leaving now?" Clint asked Lissa.

She looked up, saw the man and woman, and nodded her head.

"Oh yes," she said. "Oliver and Mrs. Graham."

"What's their interest in you?"

"Well. He's *Dr.* Oliver Graham," Lissa said, "and as his wife, Lillian just simply hates me."

"I think there's probably more to it than that," he said.

"Oh?"

"I've seen women look at women that way before," he said. "It usually has something to do with one of them being beautiful, and one not."

Lissa Sugarman looked shocked. Obviously, she was a woman who didn't define herself by her appearance, so being told she was beautiful came as a shock.

"You're saying she hates me because . . . because I'm prettier than she is?"

"Exactly."

"Well, that's just . . . ridiculous."

"It's true," he said. "I've seen it many times before."

"I'm sure . . . I'm sure it's something . . . else," she said, touching her face, and pulling her hand away quickly.

"Do you know the best thing about a beautiful woman?" he asked. "I mean, a truly beautiful woman?"

She frowned at him.

"What?"

"She doesn't know she's beautiful."

Red-faced, she said, "Well, now you're just being silly. I think we should go."

"I want my dessert," Clint said. "Besides, if we go out there now, we might come face-to-face with Dr. and Mrs. Graham. You wouldn't want that, would you?"

"Well, no . . ."

"And you wouldn't want to deprive me of my peach pie, would you?"

"Of course not."

"Good," he said. "Then let's have our coffee and dessert."

When they went outside, they drew a few looks from people on the street, but Clint put it down to Lissa's beauty.

"People are looking at you, too, you know," she said as they climbed into her buggy.

"No," he said, "they're looking at you."

She smiled, brightened, and said, "Maybe we just make a striking couple."

"That could be it," he said.

She got her horse going, turned him, and headed up the

street at a trot, expertly avoiding other wagons along the way.

"But you are the Gunsmith," she said. "Don't people recognize you on the street?"

"Sometimes," he said. "I was just hoping that wouldn't happen as often down here."

"Have you been to Veracruz before?"

"A long time ago."

She was about to ask another question when she noticed some commotion up ahead.

"Looks like an accident," she said.

Clint saw that two wagons had apparently collided. One was lying over on its side, and there seemed to be people injured.

Lissa pulled her buggy over to the side and dropped down to the ground, shouting at Clint, "Bring my bag!"

SIX

Clint reached the scene, carrying Lissa's bag. He noticed she had already hiked up her skirt and gotten down on her knees next to a couple of injured kids.

"What happened?" she asked a woman who must have been their mother.

"They were crossing the street when this runaway wagon came along," the mother said.

"It hit them?"

"No," the mother said, "another wagon tried to avoid the runaway, and that one ran over my children. Oh God, are they all right?"

"I don't know yet, ma'am," Lissa said. She looked up and reached out to Clint. "My bag!"

He hurriedly handed her the bag.

"Can I do anything else?" he asked.

"Just keep the people back."

He looked around and saw, on the other side of the wagon, that Dr. Graham was treating some people. He wondered why that doctor had not gone first to the children.

Behind Graham stood his wife, Lillian, and when she noticed Clint and Lissa, she shouted, "What is she doing here?"

"She's trying to help people!" Clint shouted back.

The woman gave him a stern look.

"She doesn't belong here!" she snapped.

"Why don't you shut up and help your husband," Clint said.

She jerked back as if he had slapped her, then bent to shout at her husband.

"Did you hear what this man said—"

"Lillian," Dr. Graham shouted, "if you're not going to help, then you *should* shut up and stand back."

Suddenly, Clint felt some respect for the doctor.

Graham abruptly looked up at him and asked, "Can you help? This man is pinned."

"Do you need me, Lissa?" he asked. "I think I can help on the other side."

"Go ahead," she said without looking up.

Clint stepped to Graham's side and saw that the man he was working on was pinned by the legs. There were no lawmen around, and bystanders were just gawking.

"These people are just staring," Graham said to Clint. "Can you get some men to help you lift the wagon so I can get this man out from beneath it?"

"Done," Clint said. He turned and didn't ask. "You, you, and you, big man, come on. Help me lift this wagon."

The big man was about six and a half feet tall and did

most of the work himself. They got the wagon up off the man's legs and Dr. Graham pulled him out.

"Clear!" he said.

They dropped the wagon back to the ground.

Now it was in the hands of both doctors. Clint saw that there were two more injured men, presumably the two drivers. They were both standing off to one side, each holding themselves where they were hurt—arm and shoulder.

So presumably, the man on the ground and the two children had been in the street, caught between the two colliding wagons.

Clint did his best to keep the people back, drafting the big man to help him. Between them they got both doctors room to work until the sheriff showed up and took over.

Finally, the doctors got their three injured patients loaded onto a buckboard. Dr. Graham's office was the closest, so they were brought there.

"Is there a hospital in Veracruz?" Clint asked Lissa.

"No," she said.

"So why don't we try to have them taken to your place?" he asked.

"Graham's is closer, he responded first, and he has more room," she said. "It's to their benefit to be taken there. That's all I'm concerned about."

Clint and Lissa turned as Dr. Graham approached them, carrying his jacket over one arm.

"Thank you for your help, Doctor," he said. "You probably saved that little girl's life."

"I was glad to help, Doctor."

Clint looked past Graham, saw his wife approaching with a furious look on her face.

"Here comes your wife," he said.

Graham rolled his eyes and said, "Thanks for the warning."

He turned and intercepted his wife before she could reach them. As he guided her away, she jerked her arm from his and started giving him an earful.

"He seems like a good doctor," Clint said.

"He is," Lissa said. "Come on, I'll take you back to your hotel."

SEVEN

When they stopped in front of Clint's hotel, he did not step down right away.

"You're a good doctor," he told her.

"All you had was a sprained foot."

"No," he said, "I'm talking about those people in the accident. You were very good with those kids."

"It's my job."

"But you love it."

"Oh, yes," she said.

"And Dr. Graham noticed it, too."

"And he's getting an earful from his wife even as we speak," she said. "That poor man."

"Are there any other doctors in town?" he asked.

"No," she said, "just him and me."

"And no hospital."

"No, but he's trying to build one."

"If he does," Clint said, "he'll need more doctors."

"If he asks," she said, "I'd have to consider it. Until then, we have our own . . . practices."

"Well," he said, stepping down, "thanks for dinner. And for fixing my foot."

"How does it feel?"

"Fine, actually," he said. "I'd forgotten all about it . . . until now."

"Well, don't forget to stay off it."

"I'll try."

He put his hand out and she took it.

"Sure you don't need help putting your buggy up?" he asked.

"I'll be fine," she said with a smile. "See you around."

"Let me know if I can help you with . . . anything," he said.

"You don't owe me anything, Clint," she said. "You paid my bill."

"That's fine," he said, "but I'll be in Veracruz for a while. Just remember, if you need me, all you have to do is ask."

"I will remember," she said. "Thanks."

He nodded. She shook the reins at her horse and headed off at a trot. He turned and went into his hotel. His foot had started to throb and he wanted to take his boot off.

While Dr. Oliver Graham went to work on the injured from the accident, his wife told him she was going home.

"I'll see you there later, dear," he said. "This might take a while."

As she left, he was thinking he certainly could have used the help of Dr. Sugarman. Once he got his hospital up and running, he wondered how he was going to explain to his wife that he was going to offer Dr. Sugarman a position.

When she left her husband, Lillian Graham did not go home. She went to a hotel not far from the one Clint was staying in. She drew looks as she walked through the lobby, not because she was beautiful—she wasn't—but because she was dressed too well for the place.

She did not stop at the front desk, but headed directly upstairs to the second floor. She walked to Room 5 and knocked. The man who opened the door was about forty, with a scarred, squared-jawed face. When he saw her, he smiled.

"Hiya, baby."

As usual, when he called her "baby," she got a chill.

"Come on in here," he said, grabbing the front of her dress and yanking her into the room.

EIGHT

His name was Rufus. He made his living by hurting people. This was something that excited some women. But he was also ugly. That was something that excited women less. So when he found a woman who was excited by him, he forgave a lot.

This doctor's wife was not attractive. She had a face like an axe, but Rufus found that if he stripped her naked and turned her over, she looked okay. She must have been in her late forties, but she had a pretty good body. And she also knew what to do in bed with a man—just lie there and let him have his way.

He knew the scars on his face had excited her from the beginning, but now after a few months he knew what else excited her.

He bunched the front of her dress in his fist, pulled her to him, and kissed her hard. Then he held her at arm's length and tore the clothes from her body. She stood there with her dress in tatters, her naked breasts heaving as she breathed hard. She had remarkably good breasts for a woman her age, full, heavy, with big brown nipples.

"Come on," she said. "I had a rough afternoon. I need this!"

He grabbed her, pawed her naked breasts, tweaked her nipples until tears came to her eyes. As good as her breasts were, it was still good to just turn her over so he wouldn't have to see her face.

He threw her on the bed, flipped her over, and removed the rest of her dress, then slapped her hard on the buttocks until they glowed red.

"Stay there!" he said.

She remained where she was, but reached for a pillow so she could bury her face in it. She didn't want anyone to hear her when she screamed.

He removed his trousers, and then his shirt. He had already been barefoot, and he never wore underwear. His cock was already swollen, but he reached down and stroked it so that it grew larger and harder. He stared at her ass while he did this. When he was sufficiently hard, he went to her, took her buttocks in both hands, and spread them. Then he leaned forward and spat on her anus. He'd learned this from a whore in Sonora. He worked his spit in with his big thumb, then pressed the spongy head of his cock there and pushed.

Lillian's screams were indeed muffled by the pillow . . .

Clint removed his boot as soon as he got into his room. He also unwrapped the foot so he could rub it. The swelling had gone down, and he hoped it would stay down. He wanted to take a walk around Veracruz the next day, see what the town looked like, maybe even go down to the docks to see what boats were coming in, and from where.

He walked slowly over to the window to look out. It was dark, and the streets were not very well lit. He could see shadows moving about, but not many of them. People in this area were probably smart enough to stay inside.

He went back to the bed and reclined, keeping his gun close. The only benefit of having hurt his foot was that he'd met Lissa Sugarman. He hoped to see more of her in the next few days.

A lot more.

She had learned to keep some clothes in Rufus's hotel room. He always tore her clothes off her. When she returned home, her husband never remembered what she had been wearing the last time he saw her.

She was sore after a couple of hours with the big ugly man. Her ass was sore from being slapped and fucked, her vagina ached, and so did her mouth and jaw. His penis was so large she sometimes thought her jaw would come unhinged, but somehow she always managed to accommodate it.

She knew she was an ugly woman, but he was an ugly man and they fit together. It excited him to brutalize a woman, and she reveled in being brutalized by him. It was something her husband would never understand.

Oliver had respect, and he had money. That was all she wanted from him. And Rufus gave her what she wanted from him, and she gave him what he wanted from a woman. And after the sex was over, they were done with each other. She had two perfect relationships with two men—one whom she dominated and one who dominated her.

In front of the hotel she got into her buggy. With any luck she'd get home before Oliver. If she didn't . . . so what?

NINE

When Clint woke the next day, he tested his ankle immediately and found it much better. Not perfect, and he knew if he spent the day on his feet, he'd pay for it by day's end, but it was better.

He got up, washed and dressed, strapped on his gun, and went downstairs to find some breakfast. The desk clerk that morning was someone he hadn't seen before, so he approached.

"Do you speak English?" he asked.

"Sí, señor," the man said, "I spik English berry good."

Well, Clint thought, good enough.

"Where is a good place to get breakfast around here?" Clint asked.

"Señor," the clerk asked, "jou are not looking for a eh-gringo breakfast, are jou?"

"No," Clint said, "a Mexican breakfast is fine."

"Ah," the man said, grinning and showing gold teeth. "Den jou go to my seester's cantina, up the street." The man pointed. "Is called Josephina's." He pronounced it *Hosephina's*.

"Josephina's," Clint repeated. "Thanks."

"De nada, señor. Please tell her that her hermano, Julio, sent you."

"I will."

Clint left the hotel, turned right, and walked up the street until he reached the cantina. He looked inside, saw about half of the dozen or so tables filled. But it was the aroma that drew him in and set his stomach to growling.

"Sit anywhere, señor," a black-haired woman called out.

Clint chose a table as far from the door and windows as he could get. The Mexican couple at the next table nodded pleasantly to him, and he returned it. He saw a small bar against one wall, but no bartender. He figured this place used to be a cantina, but had since become a restaurant.

"Excuse me?" he said once he was seated.

"Señor?" the man at the next table replied.

"Is the food good here?"

"Is best in Veracruz, señor," the man said eagerly.

"And who is that woman?" he asked, indicating the black-haired woman who had spoken to him.

"She is the owner, and the cook, señor," the man said.

"Gracias," Clint said.

"De nada, señor. Enjoy your breakfast."

He sat back and Josephina came over to his table. She wore a low-cut peasant blouse that showed off a lot of her smooth, dark skin, including full, bountiful breasts.

"Buenos días, señor," she said to him. "How can I help you?"

"With breakfast," he said.

"What would you like?"

"Whatever you recommend," he said. "I'm hungry and would like a full Mexican breakfast."

"Ah, señor," she said with a beautiful smile, "that is my specialty."

"I'm staying at the hotel down the street and your brother, Julio, told me to tell you he sent me."

"You tell my brother I am happy he sent you, but he still has to pay for his food. I will be right back, señor."

"I'll be here."

She returned with a pot of coffee and a heavy mug and poured it full for him. He tasted it and found out why the mug was so heavy and thick. Anything flimsier would have been eaten through by the coffee. It was black and strong and he loved it.

When she returned about ten minutes later, she had plates up her arms.

"Huevos rancheros," she said, putting one down, "breakfast burritos, and here are my famous jalapeño corn cakes."

"Thank you. It all looks great."

The huevos rancheros included tortillas and salsa.

He had a mouthful of huevos rancheros when the couple at the next table stood up. The man turned to face him.

"Did I not tell you, señor?"

"You did," Clint said. "It's great."

They nodded to him again and smiled, both revealing gaps where teeth used to be.

He continued to work on his breakfast and found every part of it delicious. The jalapeño corn cakes were a little hot for his taste, but still good, and he asked Josephina for another pot of her coffee.

"You have a cast-iron stomach," she said in only slightly accented English. "No one ever asks for another pot of my coffee."

"It's perfect," he said.

She brought him his second pot, and by the time he was finished, he was the only diner left in the place. Josephina came over to talk with him.

"When did you arrive in town?" she asked.

"Just yesterday," he said.

"I knew I had not seen you in here before."

"Maybe not before," he said, "but you'll be seeing me again, that's for sure."

"I am always happy to see a man who enjoys his food," she said. "But why are you staying in that terrible hotel my brother works in?"

"I was just looking for a place to lay low for a while."

"Ah, you are here because the gringo law is after you, eh?"

"No," he said, "I just wanted to go someplace where I might not be recognized."

She sat down opposite him, put her elbow on the table and her chin in her hand. The movement squeezed her breasts together so that they threatened to spill out of her blouse. He wasn't complaining. In fact, he saw a small brown semicircle of nipple aureole peeking out.

"Are you a famous man north of the border, señor?" she asked.

"Well, I guess that depends on what you mean by famous."

She waggled a finger at him.

"You are playing games," she said. "You do not want to tell me your name."

"My name is Clint."

"Just Clint?"

"Adams," he said, "Clint Adams."

She sat back, took a deep breath that swelled her breasts, and stared at him.

"Dios mío," she said. "El Armero?"

He'd heard the word translated in Spanish before, on previous visits to Mexico.

"Yes."

"My brother did not tell me he had such a famous gringo staying in the hotel."

"Well, I'm glad of that," he said. "I'd like you to keep the information to yourself."

"You do not want me to tell *anyone*?"

"No one," he said. "I'm just trying to relax for a while. If word gets out that I'm here, I'll have to leave and go somewhere else, and then you'll lose a good customer."

"Ah, then we will make a deal, eh?"

"What kind of deal?"

"I will not tell anyone that you are here," she said, "and in return, you must eat all of your meals here."

He smiled and put his hand out to shake.

"That's a deal I can live with."

TEN

Promising to return later in the day for his next meal, Clint left Josephina's and stepped outside. He'd be returning for a lot more than the food, he hoped. She seemed interested in him, and he hoped it wasn't just because he'd been the only one left in the place. She had an amazing body and he hoped to see a lot more of it.

He strolled back toward his hotel, moving slowly and favoring the ankle, which was feeling sore—though not as sore as the previous night.

When he reached the hotel, there were a couple of straight-backed wooden chairs out front, so he pulled one over and sat in it. He figured to relax and watch the town go by for a while. He usually found that if you sat in one place long enough, you could get a good feel for a town just by watching the people go by, as well as the traffic in the street.

By the same token, if you sat in one place long enough, people would sometimes get curious about you.

Three men came across the street wearing wide sombreros and bandoliers, carrying rifles. One of them had a pistol tucked into his belt. Clint had seen them going in and out of some of the businesses across the street for the better part of an hour.

And they had noticed him.

"Señor," one of them said when they reached him.

"Yes?"

"What are jou doin'?"

"Just sitting."

"Sittin' and doin' what?"

"Just watching."

The man exchanged glances with his two compadres.

"Watchin' what?"

"People," Clint said. "Just people."

"Jou been watchin' us?" the man asked.

"Are you the only one of the three who speaks English?"

"Sí."

"How did you know I spoke English?"

"Señor," the man said, "jou are a gringo, no?"

"Yes."

"And jou look like a gringo."

Clint shrugged.

"And you look like a lawman."

"And the three of you look like bandidos," Clint said. "Are you bandidos?"

"Bandidos?" the man said. "No, no, señor, we are not bandidos."

"Then why are you worried that I might be a lawman?"

"Because jou have been watchin' us, and jou might get the wrong idea."

"What idea is that?"

"About what we have been doin'."

"I assumed you were doing some shopping."

"Chopping." He looked at his amigos and said, "La compra."

The other two men laughed.

"Sí, señor," the first man said, "that is what we are doing, chopping."

"Well, that's fine, then," Clint said. "We have no problem."

"No problemo," the man said. "Sí."

"Then you fellas might as well go back to your shopping."

"And jou, señor?"

"Me? I'm just going to keep sitting here, watching the people go by."

He turned to his friends and they had a short conversation in Spanish before he turned back to Clint.

"Señor, jou are new to Veracruz, eh?"

"That's right."

"Then you should know," he said, "the people here, dey are berry boring."

"Really."

"Dey are not worth watchin' for berry long," he went on. "I think jou have seen enough."

"What are you saying?" Clint asked.

"I am sayin' dat jou should go back inside."

"I should?"

"Sí, señor."

"Or what?"

"Señor," the man said as if he was trying to be reasonable, "we are not here to threaten jou."

"Sounds like a threat to me," Clint said. "Why don't you go back to minding your own business, and I'll go back to minding mine?"

"You will continue to watch us do our eh-chopping?" the man asked.

"Well, I could," Clint said, "except that I think what you said is true about the other people is more true about you."

"What is that, señor?"

"You guys are boring."

"Boring?"

"Yes," Clint said. "With all the shopping you say you've been doing, you guys have no packages."

The spokesman turned to his friends and translated what Clint said.

"Of course," Clint said, "you could be having your items delivered."

"Señor," the man said, dropping all pretense of reasonability or amiability, "we think jou should go inside."

"And I think not," Clint said. "So where do we go from here?"

Their hands tightened on their rifles. The spokesman was the one wearing the pistol in his belt, and he put his hand on it.

"You fellas are very close to making the wrong decision," Clint said. "I just came to Veracruz and I have no desire to litter the streets with Mexican blood."

"But, señor," the man said, "we are three and jou are

one." He held up the index finger of his left hand, while keeping his right hand on his gun. "Uno."

Clint knew he could draw and shoot off the man's index finger in the blink of an eye. That would certainly send a message, and it was something he might have done many years ago, when he was younger, and brasher.

"Keep your finger there."

"Eh?" The man frowned, lowering his hand a bit.

"No, no, keep your finger up," Clint said.

"Señor?" the man said, as if confused, but he raised his finger back to where it had been.

"What's your name?"

"I am Gomez, señor."

"Well, Gomez, I'll make you a deal," Clint said. "I'll draw and fire and shoot your finger clean off. I mean, so clean it'll hardly hurt."

"Eh?"

"And if I do that, you and your friends can turn and leave. They can take you to a doctor. I know a real good one."

"Señor?"

"If I miss—and I mean, even if I hit it, but it's still dangling—I'll go inside. What do you say?"

Gomez looked at his left index finger.

"Jou are very calm, señor."

"I know."

"And jou could choot my finger off?"

"In a second."

"But we could kill you."

"I don't think so," Clint said, "but even if you do, Gomez, I'll kill you first. Then your two friends can leave us in the street and continue their shopping."

The other two men were staring at Gomez, wondering what was being said.

"Un momento, señor," Gomez said, and turned to them to translate.

Clint watched while the three men spoke. He thought the other two were kind of curious as to whether or not he could really shoot Gomez's finger off.

"Señor, jou are a berry lucky man," Gomez said.

"How's that?"

"We have decided to let you sit there as long as you want."

"That's very nice of you. I'd appreciate it if you'd take your hand off your pistol, then."

Gomez hesitated, then removed his hand.

"Good."

"Jou have a good day, señor," Gomez said.

"I will, Gomez," Clint said. "You, too."

The three men backed away, then turned and quickly walked down the street, bickering in Spanish.

They did not do any more "chopping."

ELEVEN

Dr. Oliver Graham checked on his patients. He had a small building he was hoping to make into a hospital. Right now he had all the people from the accident in beds and was keeping an eye on their progress. The two children who had been crossing the street had been seriously injured, but the quick work of Dr. Sugarman at the scene had managed to save one of the girl's legs, and the lives of both children. Of course, this made his wife very angry. She felt that Graham should have treated all three people on the street with no help, but there hadn't been time. If Dr. Sugarman had not stopped to help, the little girl would surely have lost her leg—and still might. She needed an operation, which Graham wanted to do, but his wife was telling him to ask for a lot of money for it. He felt bad for the parents, because they did not seem to have a lot of money. All he wanted to do was treat the little girl, but his wife was adamant about the money.

He was scheduled to speak with the parents this morning, and was waiting for them to arrive. He still didn't know what he was going to tell them.

He was sitting at his desk, just prior to checking on the patients again, when there was a knock at his door. He finished a notation he was making then got up and walked to the door. He was distracted as he opened it and did not see the fist coming at him. He was punched square in the face so that his nose exploded. Blood sprayed everywhere as he went windmilling back, crashed into his desk, and fell to the floor.

Someone entered, closing the door behind them. Then they approached Graham, who was sitting on the floor, trying to figure out what was going on. He couldn't see because there were blood and tears in his eyes.

"Wha-what-what's—who—" he stammered, but he couldn't speak because the blood streaming from his nose was getting into his mouth.

Suddenly, he was kicked in the chest. All the air rushed from his body and he thought he was going to die in that moment.

But he didn't.

He died several moments after that . . .

The door opened later and the parents of the two injured children entered. They immediately saw all the blood. The woman screamed, but the man assessed the situation and realized it was the doctor who was dead, not their children.

They went in search of the law.

Sheriff Kyle Brown stared down at the battered body of the doctor.

"Now who would want to do that to a sawbones?" he asked.

His deputy, Jim Boone, also stared down at the dead man.

"Maybe he overcharged somebody, Cap'n?"

Brown used to be a captain in the army. Boone never let him forget it.

"We're gonna need somebody to look after these people," Brown said.

"There is another doctor in town, Cap'n," Boone said. "That woman?"

"That's right," Brown said. "What was her name?"

"Sugar-somethin'."

"You know where her office is?"

"Just down by the docks somewhere," the deputy said. "You want I should go find her?"

"Naw," Brown said, "I'll go. You get some men to take the doctor's body to the undertaker."

"What about his wife?"

"I'll take care of that, too," Brown said. "I'll get the lady doctor to come here, and then I'll notify his wife."

"Maybe she'll know who hated him enough to beat him to death, huh?"

"Yeah," Boone said. "Maybe."

It took Kyle Brown about an hour to locate Dr. Sugarman's office. In fact, somebody told him where her office was and called her "Doc Veracruz."

"I thought her name was Sugar-somethin'," he said.

"Sí, El Jefe, but that is what some call her."

He found her office and knocked on the door, took his

hat off as she answered it. Her eyes immediately went to the badge on his chest.

"Sheriff," she said. "Can I help you?"

"I hope you can, ma'am," Sheriff Kyle Brown said. "I surely hope you can."

TWELVE

Clint spent the next two days doing the same thing. He'd get up in the morning, have breakfast at Josephina's, then go and sit in front of the hotel until it was time to go to Josephina's again for a meal.

On the evening of the second day, there was a knock at his door . . .

He was sitting up in bed, his boots off, resting his foot. He pulled his gun from the holster hanging nearby and called out, "Come in."

The door opened and Josephina stepped in, closing it behind her.

"Josephina," he said. "What brings you here? Is everything all right at the cantina?"

"Everything is fine," she said, "except for one thing."

"What's that?"

"You only come there to eat," she said. "I keep waiting

for you to come there for me, but no. All you do is eat. Am I not pretty?"

"You're not pretty," he said. "You're beautiful."

"Then why do you not come for me?"

"I was waiting," he said.

"Waiting for what?"

He smiled.

"Hijo de un cabrón!" she said in wonder. "You were waiting for me to come to you?"

"And you have."

"You are a bad man."

"Do you want to leave?"

"Oh no," she said. "Now that I am here, I am going to get what I came for."

"Be gentle," he said, pointing to his ankle, "I'm an injured man."

"You just lie back," she said, dropping her shawl from her shoulders, "and let Josephina have her fun."

The peasant blouse came off quickly, her large breasts bobbing into view, the dark brown nipples already hard. The skirt came next, kicked into a corner gracefully. She approached the bed naked, and he could feel the heat emanating from her body.

She leaned over him, ran her hand down his chest, then began to unbutton his shirt. When he started to reach for her breasts, she slapped his hands away.

"Be still!" she said.

"Yes, ma'am."

She unbuttoned his shirt and removed it, then ran her hands down his bare chest until she reached his belt buckle. She undid the buckle and buttons and removed his trousers, sliding them down his legs along with his underwear. Now he was naked, his penis standing straight and begging for her attention.

She took his penis first in one hand, then in two, slowly stroking it while licking her lips.

"I am not a whore, señor, but I know certain things—" she started.

"Don't worry about a thing, Josephina," he said. "You do whatever you want."

She made a sound like "Mmmmm," as when something tastes good, then swooped in and took his penis into her mouth. She wet the head of his dick thoroughly, licking and sucking it, then lowered her mouth until most of his shaft was inside, where it was steamy hot. As she leaned into him, her nipples brushed his thighs. She rode him with her mouth, and as he snuck a hand in to take gentle hold of her breast, she allowed it. She became more and more avid, until finally she released her lips and got on the bed with him. She mounted him, reached down to hold him steady, and sat down on him, taking his cock inside. If her mouth had been hot, now she was burning like fire. She pressed her hands flat against his chest, leaned forward, and began to ride him. Her eyes were closed and she was lost in her own pleasure. She had really meant it when she said she was going to have her fun, but as he slid his hands beneath her ass, he figured there was no harm in him having some fun, too . . .

He was sitting in front of the hotel, replaying the night in his mind, when a small boy approached him, almost shyly.

"Sir?"

"Yes?"

"Are you Clint Adams?"

"That's right."

"Es verdad?" the boy asked. "The Gunsmith? La Leyenda?"

"Yes."

"Gee . . . a lady gave me a note, said you'd give me two bits when I delivered it."

"Two bits, huh?"

"Yes."

He handed the boy the coin thinking, I guess there are no discounts for legends.

THIRTEEN

When Clint got to Dr. Oliver Graham's office, he found Lissa Sugarman very busy.

"All the victims of that accident are here," she told him. "Please have a seat and I'll be right with you."

He sat down, wondering what one doctor was doing in the other doctor's office. When he looked down at the floor, he thought he saw his answer. Someone had scrubbed, but they couldn't get all the blood out.

When she came back in, she said, "I'm sorry, I've been here for a couple of hours and already . . ."

"What happened here?" he asked, indicating the blood.

"Dr. Graham was found beaten to death this morning," she said.

"And how did you get here?"

"The sheriff came and asked me if I'd see to his patients. There's no other doctor in town."

"I'm sure that's adding insult to injury for his wife," he

said. "Why did you send me a message saying you needed my help?"

She pushed a lock of hair out of her face and sat down opposite him, folding her hands into her lap.

"I'm afraid."

"Of what?"

"I think the sheriff thinks I did this."

"What?"

"It makes sense," she said. "Who benefits most from the death of Dr. Graham? Me."

"How about his wife?" Clint asked. "She gets everything now that he's dead, right?"

"I don't like the way the sheriff was looking at me," she said.

"Has he said anything about suspecting you?"

"No."

"All right, what's his name?"

"Brown," she said. "Sheriff Kyle Brown."

"I don't know him," he said, "and I don't know the name, but I'll stop in and have a talk with him."

She breathed a sigh of relief.

"Thank you," she said. "I didn't know who else to go to for help."

"Well," he said, "I told you to come find me if you needed me." He stood up. "How are the patients?"

"I had to do some surgery this morning on the little girl to try and save her leg."

"Did you do it?"

"I did the surgery," she said, "but it remains to be seen if I can restore circulation to her right leg and save it."

"How old is she?"

"Six."

"I hope you can do it."

"So do I. I'll have to watch her all day."

Clint wondered what would happen if the sheriff decided to arrest Lissa. Would he hold off until the little girl was out of danger?

"What are you going to do for food later?" he said.

"I'll try to have something right here."

"I'll bring something back with me after I see the sheriff," Clint said. "We can eat together."

"All right. Thank you."

"You just worry about the patients," he said, "and I'll worry about the sheriff."

"It's a deal," she said.

He patted her shoulder, and then she went back to check on her patients as he left the office.

FOURTEEN

Clint found the sheriff's office with no problem. He entered, saw three armed men wearing badges standing around a desk. They all looked at him.

"Sheriff Brown?" he asked.

He expected the older of the three men to step forward, but it was the middle one. He stepped forward while the other two simply turned their heads.

"I'm Brown."

"Can I talk to you a minute?"

"About what?"

"Oliver Graham."

"Dr. Graham?"

"That's right."

The two deputies turned to face him now.

"You know Graham?"

"Not really."

"Then what do you know?"

"I know Dr. Sugarman."

"Mister, who are you?"

"A friend of Dr. Sugarman's," Clint said. "My name's Clint Adams."

"Clint Adams?" Brown repeated.

"That's right."

"The Gunsmith?" the older deputy asked. "That Clint Adams?"

"That's right."

"Gee," the young deputy said, his eyes going wide.

The sheriff turned to the older deputy.

"Jim, take Ed out and show him the rounds."

"Sure, Cap'n."

Both deputies donned their hats and left the office.

"New deputy?" Clint asked.

"Brand new," Brown said. "Have a seat, Mr. Adams. I'd offer you some coffee but I'm fresh out."

"No problem."

Clint sat. Brown went around behind his desk and sat down.

"Why do you want to talk about Dr. Sugarman?" he asked.

"She's kind of worried."

"About what?"

"Somebody in town killed a doctor," Clint said. "That leaves one doctor in town. Her."

"So?"

"So she's worried the killer might come after her next," Clint said. "You got any reason to think that might happen?"

"None."

"Okay, then." Clint stood up.

"That's it?" the lawman asked.

"Sure," Clint said. "I just had the one question."

"Well, sit back down, Mr. Adams," Brown said. "I got some questions for you."

Clint was impressed by the lawman. He looked about forty, didn't seem to be impressed by Clint's reputation. Or if he was, he was hiding it well.

He sat back down.

"What do you know about Drs. Graham and Sugarman?" the sheriff asked.

"Not much. I met them both when I came to town."

"When was that?"

"Couple of days ago."

"I thought you said you were a friend of Dr. Sugarman's?"

"I make friends fast."

"But not with Graham?"

"Well, we didn't really meet," Clint said. "I helped him get a man out from under a wagon that had turned over on the street."

"I know about that accident," Brown said. "Dr. Sugarman was there, too."

"Yes, she was with me. When we saw what was happening, we went to help."

"And that was the first time she met Dr. Graham?"

"As far as I know."

"Tell me something, Mr. Adams," Brown said. "Why does Dr. Sugarman have an office down by the docks?"

"I suppose it's because she wants to be there," Clint replied.

"Nobody wants to be down there."

"Well, she's just starting out here in Veracruz, and she said she wanted to be where people needed her."

"You got any reason to think Dr. Sugarman might have wanted to kill Dr. Graham?"

Clint frowned at the man.

"I thought he was beaten to death. Do you really think—"

"How do you know that?"

"What?"

"How do you know that? I didn't say how he was killed. In fact, how did you know he was killed?"

"I stopped by his office today. I wanted to see how those people were. Imagine my surprise to see blood on the floor, and Dr. Sugarman there."

"So you decided to come over here and talk to me?"

"I did when Dr. Sugarman told me about her fears," Clint said.

"So you don't believe Dr. Sugarman would've killed him—or had him killed—so she could take over his practice?"

"That sounds ridiculous."

"Does it? A good medical practice can be worth a lot of money."

"In Veracruz?"

"Veracruz is growing," Brown said. "Doc Graham was gonna open a hospital."

"Well, I don't think she had anything to do with it, Sheriff."

"Why not? Because she's a woman?"

"She just doesn't seem to be that kind of person."

"Anybody can commit murder, Mr. Adams, given the right circumstances."

Clint stood up.

"Well, I don't think those circumstances exist here. Mind if I go now?"

"Where are you staying?"

Clint told him.

"I'm gonna stay in touch with you, if you don't mind."

"I don't mind at all, Sheriff," Clint said. "If you think I can help you, let me know."

"I'll do that. Meanwhile, why don't you put the good doctor's mind at ease and tell her I don't have any reason to believe someone is targeting doctors. Not at the moment anyway."

"I'll tell her, Sheriff. Thanks."

FIFTEEN

Clint stopped off for some tacos and enchiladas, brought them over to Dr. Graham's office in a basket. He wished he could have bought them from Josephina's, but her place was just too far away. No point in going all the way there and then all the way back.

He entered the office, found it empty. Lissa must have been checking on the patients again. He had the food out and on plates on Dr. Graham's desk when she came back into the room.

"Wow, I could smell that from the other room. Thanks. I'm starved."

"I don't have anything to drink with it," he said.

"Coffeepot over there."

"I'll make it. How's the little girl?"

"She's good. She's got good color back in her leg. She should have some feeling in it by tomorrow."

"So you did a good job, huh?"

She bit into a taco and said, "I did a helluva job—and so did you. This is great."

He put the coffee on and then joined her at the desk, sitting across from her. He grabbed a taco and bit into it. Not as good as Josephina's, but good nevertheless.

"Did you see the sheriff?" she asked.

"I did," Clint said.

"What did he say?"

"Well, I didn't ask him the question straight out," Clint replied. "I told him you were worried the killer might be killing doctors. He said he had no reason to believe that."

"That was a smart way to approach him," she said. "I'm impressed."

"Well, we finally did move on to the subject you're actually interested in."

"And?"

"He seems to think you're one of the people who might benefit from the doctor's death."

"Who else?"

"Well . . ."

"He didn't mention anyone else, did he?" She put down the taco she'd been eating, as if she'd just lost her appetite.

"No, he didn't," Clint said, "but I'm sure that Graham's wife, at least, is a suspect."

"Yeah, maybe number two on his list."

"I'll just have to make her number one on my list," Clint said.

"What? You're going to investigate?"

"I don't know if I'd call it that," he said. "But I do have some friends who are very good detectives, and I've worked with them. I've learned from them that the best way to find out answers is to ask questions. So that's what I'm going to do."

"I don't know how to thank you." She picked up her half-eaten taco and took a bite. "What will you be doing first?"

"Well, if I make his wife my number one suspect, I'll have to talk to her," Clint said. "If she didn't do it, she might have an idea who did."

"Maybe she has a lover," Lissa said.

"Hmm, did you see her the other day?" he asked. "I can't imagine she'd have a lover."

"Why not?" Lissa asked. "There's somebody for everybody."

"Still . . ."

"Don't be unkind, Clint," she said, picking up another taco.

"That woman may be your only out," he said, "and you don't want me to be unkind? You're an amazing woman, Lissa."

"I hardly think . . ." She trailed off, looking embarrassed. "Do you think the sheriff might come for me?" she asked, changing the subject.

"I doubt it," Clint said. "There'd be nobody else to take care of these people. By the way, didn't Dr. Graham have a nurse?"

"I—I don't know," she said, looking shocked that she hadn't asked. "I haven't seen one all day."

"I'll ask his wife about that, too," he said. "Let me get that coffee."

He poured two cups and handed her one, then sat down and started in on an enchilada.

"I could use a nurse here, now that you mention it," she said. "I'd like to have a bath and collect some clothes from home. I think I should be staying here for a few days."

"What would a nurse have to do?" he asked.

"Just monitor the patients," she said. "Give them some water if they want it."

"That's all?"

"Well, a little more, but I wouldn't be gone that long. Monitoring their vital signs would be most important."

"Monitoring vital signs?"

"Watching for a rise in their temperature, taking their pulse, things like that."

"Could I do it?"

"Well . . . it's not simple, but . . . you seem like a smart man."

He frowned and she laughed.

"How about I go and talk to Mrs. Graham, and then after that I'll come back here and let you go for a little while."

"Well," she said, "if Mrs. Graham mentions a nurse, you can come back with her. Otherwise, I'll show you a few things and take you up on your offer."

"Okay," he said. "More coffee and another taco and I'll be on my way."

As he reached for a taco, she reached out and touched his hand.

"I don't know how I'll ever be able to thank you for your help."

"Hey," he said, "my foot feels a lot better. That's thanks enough."

She shook her head but didn't argue.

SIXTEEN

Clint found Dr. Graham's address in the dead man's desk. He left the office and headed back to the docks to retrieve Eclipse from the livery. He rode the big Darley Arabian to the better part of town, where he matched the address up to a big two-story house with white columns out front. As he dismounted and looped Eclipse's reins around a pole, he thought—to his mind anyway—Mrs. Graham's motive for murdering her husband, or for having him murdered, had just gotten stronger. Maybe she was worried he was going to use too much of his own money to start up his hospital.

He mounted the front steps and knocked on the huge ornate front door. When it opened, he found himself looking at the woman from the restaurant, Mrs. Graham. She still had a hatchet face, but the dress she was wearing showed that she had a good body for a woman her age, which he figured to be late forties. Maybe the idea that she had a lover wasn't so far-fetched after all.

"Yes?"

"Mrs. Graham?" he said. "My name is Clint Adams."

She frowned.

"I've seen you—yes, in the street the other day. You helped lift that buckboard off my husband's patient."

"That's right."

"What do you want here?" she demanded.

"Just a talk."

"About what?"

"Your husband's death."

"Do you know something about that?"

"I don't know anything about it," he said, "but that's what I'm trying to find out."

"Are you working with the sheriff?"

Instead of answering truthfully, he said, "I just came from Sheriff Brown's office," to see if that would get him through the front door.

It did.

"Very well," she said. "Come inside."

Clint entered, and she left it to him to close the door and then follow her. She led him into a plushly furnished living room. If she spent this much money on furniture, he thought, she probably wouldn't want her husband spending it elsewhere.

"What can I do for you, Mr. . . . Adams, did you say?" she asked.

"That's right." She didn't seem to recognize his name. That was fine with him.

"Well, have a seat and say what you've come to say." She sat on the sofa. He chose an armchair across from her. When he sat, he felt like he was going to sink out of sight.

"First, I'd like to say I'm sorry for your loss."

"Yes, yes," she said, "I've been hearing that from everyone. What questions do you have for me, Mr. Adams?"

"Well, first, do you know anyone who might have wanted to kill your husband?"

"The sheriff asked me that," she said. "No, I don't."

"Are you sure?" Clint asked. "He never came home and said someone threatened him?"

"No."

Clint looked around.

"This is quite an expensive house, isn't it?"

"Yes, it is."

"Who gets it, now that your husband's dead?"

"Why, I do, of course."

"And your husband's money?"

"I get that, too," she said. "Mr. Adams, are you trying to insinuate that I killed my husband? Do you think I marched into his office and beat him to death?" She raised her hands. "With these?"

"No," he said, "of course not."

She lowered her hands. "Of course not."

"But you could have hired somebody to do it."

"Why would I do that?"

"I got the impression, when I saw the two of you together, that you didn't quite get along."

"We got along fine."

"As long as he did what you said, right?"

"I am not a woman easily dominated, Mr. Adams," she said. She thought the comment was ironic, but this man had no idea of the irony. "And my husband was a man who needed to be dominated."

"Is that a fact?"

"It is."

"Do you think he saw it that way?"

"To tell you the truth, Mr. Adams, I really never cared how he saw it," she said.

"You're a hard woman, Mrs. Graham."

"That's right, I am, Mr. Adams," she said. "I think it's time for you to leave."

He stood up.

"Before I go, did your husband have a nurse?"

"He did, for a while, lovely young girl named Marietta."

"What happened to her?"

"I fired her."

"You fired her?"

"That's right."

"What gave you the right to fire her?"

She smiled.

"I gave myself the right," she said. "She was too . . . pretty."

"Young and pretty, huh?"

"That's right."

"Was she a good nurse?"

"I didn't care."

"Great," he said. "They need a nurse at your husband's office."

"His office? What are you talking about?"

"There are still patients there," he said. "The doctor looking after them needs a nurse."

"Doctor? What doctor? The only other doctor in town is . . . that bitch? She's in Oliver's office?"

"That's right."

"By what right?"

"The sheriff asked her to look after the patients."

"That's . . . impossible."

"Do you know where I can find Marietta, the nurse?"

"No," Lillian Graham said. "And I don't care. You tell that woman to get out of my husband's office."

"If I did that, ma'am," he asked, "who would take care of those people?"

"I don't care!" she shouted. "I want her out!"

"You'll have to take that up with the law, Mrs. Graham," Clint said. "Now, if you'll excuse me . . ."

He turned and left the house.

Lillian stood there for a few moments after Clint Adams left, trembling with rage. She didn't move until Rufus came down. He stood in the doorway, naked, his huge penis and balls dangling down.

"You comin' upstairs, baby?" he asked.

She looked at him. He was huge and hairy.

"I have something I'd like you to do," she said.

"Well, come upstairs and I'll do it."

"Oh, we'll do that, too," she said, "but after, I need you to do something for me."

"Okay," he said, "but first you do somethin' for me."

He walked up to her, grabbed the front of her dress in his left paw, and tore it from her. Her breasts came into view, pale and kind of saggy. He'd always known they were kind of saggy, but they seemed even more so today. Once he had his hands on some of her husband's money, he'd be able to buy himself some women with perky breasts. But for now . . .

He pushed her down to her knees.

"Wait," she said.

"I don't wait," he said. "Ain't that why you like havin' me around?"

He reached down and massaged his prick until it started to rise up.

"Come on, now," he said. "Be a good girl and open your mouth."

She was kinda ugly, but she had a hot mouth. He stuck his dick in, grabbed the back of her head, and started to fuck her mouth.

Damn it, she thought, she was getting wet between her legs. She couldn't resist him when he treated her this way. She opened her mouth wider and took him in.

"That's nice, real nice," he said as she sucked him.

Later, she thought, she'd have him go to the office and throw that bitch out.

She reached between her legs with one hand and touched herself while she took hold of him with the other hand and stroked him, all the while still sucking.

SEVENTEEN

Clint rode back to the doctor's office.

"Did you talk to her?" Lissa asked as he entered.

"I did," he said. "That's one hard woman."

"What did she say?"

"Enough to convince me that she had her husband killed," he said.

"Can you prove it?"

"Not right now," he said. "I'm going to work on it, but first there's something else I have to do."

"What's that?"

"Get you your nurse."

"He had one?"

"Once," he said, "but his wife fired her."

"Oh, my. Do you know who she is?"

"I have a first name," he said. "Marietta. There should be a file here someplace with her last name, and address."

"I saw some files here," she said, opening a drawer.

She leafed through them, then pulled a folder out and read the name off of it.

"Marietta Gonzales."

"Write her address down for me," he said. "I'll go tell her she has her job back, if she wants it."

She wrote it down and handed it to him.

"Who's going to pay her?"

"We can worry about that later. Do you want me to stay awhile so you can go and have that bath?"

"No," she said, "it would take me too long to show you what to do. Why don't you go and see if Miss Gonzales even wants her job back. If she does, you can bring her back here. Then I can go."

"Okay."

"Do you know where that is?" she asked, indicating the piece of paper in his hand.

"I'll find it," he said. "Be back soon."

He had to ask directions, but he eventually knocked on the door of Marietta Gonzales's house. It was on the totally opposite side of town from Dr. Graham's home.

The man who answered the door was in his late thirties, very tall but out of shape. He had a potbelly, was balding, and was wiping the greasy fingers of one hand on his shirt. In the other he held a huge chicken leg.

"Qué pasa?" he asked.

"You speak English?"

"Sí," the man said, "I spik English. What do jou want?"

"Does Marietta live here?"

"Who are jou?"

"My name is Clint Adams."

"What do jou want with my Marietta?" the man demanded, frowning.

"I want to give her her job back."

The man's face brightened. He turned and shouted over his shoulder, "Marietta!"

Clint walked back into the office with Marietta Gonzales in tow. She was younger than her husband, early twenties, small and pretty. He'd gotten the distinct impression she'd either been given or sold to the man.

"Marietta," he said, "this is Dr. Sugarman."

The girl's eyes widened.

"Dios mío. Jou are a woman."

"Yes, I am," Lissa said, "and you are a nurse?"

"I was Dr. Graham's nurse."

"Do you have training?"

"Dr. Graham," she said nervously, "he—he trained me himself."

"Well, come with me, Marietta," Lissa said, "and let's see how good a job he did."

"Sí, señora."

"Doctor," Lissa said, "just call me Doctor."

"Sí, Doctor."

"See you later, Clint," Lissa said, "and thanks."

Rufus took Lillian Graham, now fully naked, upstairs and threw her on the bed. He got her on her hands and knees and took her from behind. He couldn't wait until he could buy himself a woman he could take from the front without having to cover her face. Lillian had been good enough for him for a while, but now that she was going to have her husband's money, and he didn't have to stay in that fleabag hotel anymore, things were going to change.

But she still had one thing for him to do before he could get some money from her, and she'd tell him what it was as soon as he finished tearing her up from behind.

EIGHTEEN

When Clint walked into the sheriff's office, the older deputy, Jim Boone, was the only one there.

"Mr. Adams," he said with a nod. He was standing, not sitting, behind his boss's desk.

"Deputy," Clint said. "Sheriff around?"

"Not right now," Boone said. "Fact is, I ain't sure where he is right now. Somethin' I can do to help you?"

"I had a talk with him about the Dr. Graham murder," Clint said. "Told him I was going to talk to the widow."

Boone's eyebrows went up.

"That's a hard woman," he said.

"Exactly what I was thinking. Do you know if the sheriff is considering that she might have hired someone to do it?" Clint asked.

"I think he's leanin' towards that other doctor, the woman, uh, Sugarman?"

"Then why would he put her in Graham's office, taking care of his patients?"

Boone shrugged.

"Somebody's gotta take care of 'em, and he sure knows where she is now."

"Two good points."

"So you think the wife did it?"

"That's a big house, and I presume there's a lot of money involved. She might have had a lover—"

"Uh, you said you talked to the widow?" Boone asked. "Did you see her?"

"Like somebody told me," Clint said, "there's somebody for everybody."

"I guess . . ."

"How well did you know the doctor?"

"Not at all," Boone said. "I never met him."

"You never had to go to him?"

"I don't get sick."

"What about injuries?"

"I usually take care of them myself," he said.

Clint knew what the man meant. He was of a generation—Clint's generation—that knew how to take care of themselves, knew how to remove a bullet and stitch a wound.

"When you see your boss, tell him I talked with the widow and I think she might have had her husband killed."

"I'll tell him. You, uh, gonna stay in town until we find out the truth?"

"Yep."

"You know the lady doctor?"

"I met her when I first came to town," Clint said. "I hurt my ankle on the trail, wasn't sure if it was broke or not."

"And?"

"It's not."

"That's good."

"But that's when I met her, and I like her," Clint said. "I don't think she was after Graham's practice. I think she wants to build her own."

"Well," Boone said, "I guess she's got his now, whether she wanted it or not."

"I guess so," Clint said, "but the widow's not happy. She wants Doc Sugarman out of her husband's office."

"Then who'd take care of the patients?"

"She doesn't care about that."

"Like I said," Boone said. "Hard woman."

"I got Doc Sugarman a nurse to work with her."

"Where'd you find a nurse?"

"A young Mexican girl who Doc Graham had trained. She worked for him until the doctor's wife fired her for being too young and pretty."

"Seems like those patients are gonna be well cared for, at least for a while."

"Looks like it," Clint said. "The doc has already saved one little girl's leg."

"That's good."

"How's your new deputy working out?"

Boone made a face,

"He's too young, but nobody else wants the job . . . unless . . . ?"

"No, not me," Clint said. "My badge-wearing days are long behind me."

"We could sure use you."

"I'll be around," Clint said. "If you need help, let me know, but I'm not going to put on a badge."

"Suit yourself," Boone said with a shrug. "This kid ain't gonna last too long. He's already struttin' too much behind that star we pinned on him."

"Maybe he'll learn."

"Yeah, he'll learn by gettin' dead."

"You and the sheriff seem to know what you're doing," Clint said.

"Yeah, well, we been at it for a while."

"How long have you been his deputy?"

"Three years."

"I would have thought it'd be the other way around, you being older and all."

"It was the other way around," Boone said. "He was my deputy until he beat me in the election three years ago."

"And you stayed on as his deputy?"

"First order of business when he won was to ask me to be his deputy," Boone said. "We had worked together well for two years before that. I like Veracruz, didn't want to leave, don't know nothin' else but wearin' a badge. I got to stay on, and he ended up with the headaches. It's been a good deal for me."

"No ego?" Clint asked.

"I got an ego, but that didn't mean nothin' in this case," Boone said. "We work together about the same, 'cept like I said, the headaches are his. He has to play the political game, I don't."

"I get what you mean," Clint said. "That was always my least favorite part of the job."

"I'll tell the sheriff you stopped by," Boone promised.

"Okay," Clint said. "I'll stop by later, maybe catch him in."

"Good talkin' to ya," Deputy Boone said.

"Same here."

NINETEEN

Clint decided to talk to some of the people who had businesses around Dr. Graham's office. His friend Talbot Roper was the best private detective he'd ever met, and it was he who told Clint that the only way to find the answers was "to ask the right people the right questions."

So he spent the rest of the day talking to people, though there really wasn't that much left of the day. Much of it had been spent retrieving Eclipse from the livery and then bringing him back there.

Basically, he wanted to know if anyone had seen somebody suspicious hanging around the doctor's office. Or if anyone had seen the doctor's wife in the company of somebody suspicious.

He stopped in a store across the street from the doctor's office just as a woman was pulling the shade down on the front door.

"Can I just talk to you for a minute?" he asked the

middle-aged woman. This would be his last stop of the day, because all the businesses were closing up.

She sighed, looked put-upon, then opened her door a crack.

"This is a hat shop, sir, not a hardware store," she said. "I hardly think I have anything in here that would interest you."

"I'm really not interested in shopping," Clint said.

"Well, then, what do you think I can do for you?" she asked.

"I'd like to talk to you about the murder of Dr. Graham, across the street."

Her eyes widened with interest and she immediately swung the door open.

"Come in, come in," she said. "I suppose I can make time for a good cause. That poor man didn't deserve to die like that."

She shut the door after he'd entered, put her closed sign in the window, and pulled the shade down. The last thing she did was turn the lock. It was odd, but Clint suddenly felt trapped.

"Would you like some tea?" she asked. "I always have a cup of tea after I've closed."

"That would be nice."

"Come with me."

The woman was about Lillian Graham's age, late forties, pleasant-faced but a bit chubby, with wide hips and a large butt. Clint followed her through a curtained doorway and found himself in a small kitchen. Through another doorway he saw some furniture.

"Do you live here?"

"Yes, I do," she said. "It's difficult to run a business and maintain a home elsewhere. My name is Gloria Wells, by the way."

"Miss Wells. I'm Clint Adams."

"What is your interest in Dr. Graham's death, Mr. Adams?" she asked.

"I'm just trying to help find out who killed him, ma'am."

She said, "Humph," and put the kettle on the stove. Clint suspected this woman had something she desperately wanted to talk about, which was probably the reason she had let him in. He decided to wait until they were sitting, having tea and cookies, before he gave her the chance.

"Miss Wells—"

"Missus," she corrected. "I'm a widow."

"Oh, I'm sorry," he said.

"That's all right," she said. "Mr. Wells went quickly two years ago. We had thirty wonderful years together."

"Well, that's good," I said.

"Not like some people."

"Some people?" he asked. "Which people are those?"

"Well," she said, "I don't like to speak ill of the dead, but the doctor and his wife did not have a very happy marriage."

"How so?"

"Well, if you'll pardon my French—"

"Of course."

"She was always such a royal bitch to him."

"I see. And that was obvious?"

"To anyone with eyes," she said.

"So he mistreated her?" Clint asked, purposely turning it around.

"Hell no," she said. Then she added, "Excuse me."

"Sure."

"She mistreated him," Gloria said.

"I see."

"In fact," she said, "it wouldn't surprise me if she had him killed."

"Did you ever see her with another man?"

"Well . . ."

"You have?"

"I saw her, once, coming out of a hotel . . . with a man."

"Really?" He found that very interesting. "Where was this hotel?"

"In a not very nice section of town."

"Could you give me directions?"

"Of course," she said, and did. She gave him very good directions.

"And what made you think that anything was . . . going on?" he asked.

"The man she was with was a big, younger, hulking brute of a man," Gloria Wells said, "not at all like her husband."

"I see."

She sipped her tea.

"Gloria?"

"Yes?"

"What were you doing in that part of town?"

"I was . . . just passing by."

Clint picked up his teacup. He looked at Gloria over

the rim. He could certainly see where she might have been there with her own hulking brute.

It actually made more sense to him than Lillian Graham being there.

TWENTY

He left Gloria Wells's store, wondering if she had been doing just what she'd accused Lillian Graham of doing—except that Gloria had no husband to answer to. Maybe Graham found out that his wife had a lover. Maybe they had a fight and it got out of hand. It was doubtful she had beaten him to death herself, so maybe she had her lover do it. And maybe the lover was in it for the money. He could certainly believe that a man would be carrying on with Lillian in order to get his hands on her husband's money.

He stopped just in front of the store and looked around. Closed signs were showing in all the windows. There were people on the streets, most of them probably heading home. Then he saw the man.

He was a big fellow, lots of black hair, sloping shoulders, thick through the middle. What had Gloria said about the man Lillian had been with? A brute? This man sure matched that description.

Clint moved sideways, then into the deep doorway of the shop next to Gloria's. He watched the big man, who was showing interest in the building that housed Graham's office.

The man walked back and forth in front of the building. Maybe he was trying to decide whether or not to go in and see the doctor. Or maybe it was something else entirely.

In the end, the man decided not to enter the building. Instead, he walked away down the street. Clint decided to follow him.

The man walked with giant strides, and Clint felt himself having to hurry to keep up. Ultimately, he took Clint right where he wanted to go—the docks. They even went past Clint's hotel, the livery where Eclipse was staying, then finally to a hotel that—when he checked his directions—matched the description of the hotel Gloria Wells had described to him.

He looked across the street, where there was another fleabag hotel. Had Gloria been coming out of that one when she saw Lillian coming out of this one? Well, that was her business.

His business was this hotel in front of him, and the man who had gone inside.

He started into the hotel, stopped when he saw a woman coming out. She smiled at him, looked him up and down, and he knew the offer was coming.

"Lookin' for me, sweetie?"

She had a lot of makeup on, including a drawn-on beauty mark above her upper lip. There might have been a pretty woman underneath, but he really couldn't tell.

Her dress was cut low enough to show her breasts, which didn't have as much bounce to them as they probably once had.

"I wish I was, darling," he said, "but I've got some business to attend to. Maybe later?"

"I'll be around," she said, "but what kind of business does a good-lookin' man like you have in a sorry dump like this?"

"Not here, but I thought I just saw a friend of mine go in here," he said. "Great big fella, lots of black hair—"

"You're friends with Rufus?"

"Rufus . . . who?"

"Big ugly fella who just walked in here," she said. "He has a room. Don't know his last name."

"One of your customers?"

She laughed. "He wishes. He don't have enough money to afford me. He's got him a woman."

"Another, uh, lady of the evening like you?"

"Hell, no," she said. "Hatchet-faced old biddy who probably likes it rough."

"Rough?"

"I can hear her screamin' through the walls when she's with him," she said. "I think them two probably deserve each other."

"Doesn't sound like the man I thought it was," Clint said. "Thanks a lot."

"Remember me, honey," she said. "Name's Wanda."

"I won't forget you, Wanda."

She waggled the fingers of her right hand at him and flounced down the street, toward the docks.

Clint backed away from the hotel, walked across the

street, and found a doorway. He needed some time to think.

He himself had thought of Lillian Graham as "hatchet-faced," and that was exactly how Wanda had described Rufus's woman. He supposed a woman married to a respectable doctor could have the urge for some rough sex with a man like Rufus.

He left his doorway and went back across the street to the hotel. This time he entered and approached the desk.

"Help ya?" a bored young clerk asked.

"I'm looking for a fella I met last night, played poker, and he owes me money. All I know is he lives in a hotel down here someplace."

"I don't know nothin'."

Clint took a dollar from his pocket and laid it on the desk.

"All I know is his name's Rufus," Clint said. "I'm just looking for where he lives, and what his last name is."

The man eyed Clint, then grabbed the dollar and closed his fist around it.

"We got a Rufus Holmes livin' here."

"Big fella?"

"Real big," the kid said.

"How's he make his living?" Clint asked.

Clint put four bits on the bar.

"That's it," he said to the kid, who snatched it up.

"He hurts people."

"What?"

"He gets paid to hurt people," the clerk said.

"I get it," Clint said. "What do you know about a woman who comes here to see him?"

"What's that got to do with him owin' you money?" the kid asked. Clint just gave him a hard look. "Okay, okay, he's got some highfalutin lady slummin' down here with him. She goes to his room, does a lot of screamin', then comes down and leaves."

"Don't know who she is?"

"No idea, but damn, she's ugly. He'd do better with any of these whores."

"But then he'd have to pay them."

"Guess you're right." Then the kid's eyes lit up. "Hey, you think she's payin' *him*?"

"Could be."

Suddenly, the kid looked like he had more respect for Rufus.

"Okay, thanks," Clint said.

"Sure."

Clint started to leave.

"Hey, mister?" the kid called.

"Yeah?" Clint turned.

"You mind if I tell him you was lookin' for him?" the clerk asked.

Clint knew the kid thought he might be able to sell Rufus the information.

"Why not?" Clint said. "Go ahead and make yourself some extra money."

"Hey, thanks, mister."

Clint said, "Don't mention it," and left the hotel.

TWENTY-ONE

"Buy you a drink?"

Boone looked up from his boss's desk. This time he was sitting behind it.

"Still lookin' for the sheriff?"

"No, looking for you this time. I want to buy you a drink and pick your brain."

"Okay," Boone said. "I never turn down a free drink." He stood up, grabbed his hat and gun. "But I pick the place."

"Sure," Clint said. "You know the town better than I do. In fact, that's why I want to talk to you."

"Okay," Boone said. "Drink first, talk after."

"Lead the way."

Clint expected Deputy Boone to take him to some noisy, smoke-filled saloon with girls and gambling, but he was surprised when the man led him to a small place with a bar and a few tables.

"My favorite place to drink," he said as they entered, "and think."

"Quiet."

"That's the point."

They walked to the bar and the bartender smiled.

"Hey, Jim."

"Tom," Boone said. "Meet my friend, Clint Adams."

"Hello, Mr. Adams. What'll it be?"

"I'll have a beer," Clint said.

"Jim?"

"Since my friend's paying, I'll have a whiskey and a beer."

"Comin' up, gents."

Clint looked around. There were others there, but no one was talking to anyone.

"Everyone who comes here keeps his own counsel," Boone said.

"Are they going to be mad if we have a conversation?" Clint asked.

"It's up to each individual whether they talk or not," Boone said.

"Here ya go, gents," the bartender said.

"Thanks, Tom."

Boone downed the whiskey in one shot, then sipped his beer.

"What's on your mind?" Boone asked.

Clint swallowed some beer.

"Do you know a man named Rufus Holmes?"

"Oh, yeah, I know Rufus," Boone said. "How did you meet him?"

"I haven't met him," Clint said, "but I've come across him."

"How?"

"He's Lillian Graham's lover."

Boone stared at him.

"No."

"Yes."

"But she's so . . . and he's so . . ."

"Ugly?"

Boone scratched his head.

"I don't know," the deputy said. "I guess that could make sense. And Rufus could be after her for the money."

"Which means he killed her husband for her?" Clint suggested.

"Or on his own," Boone said. "Or not at all. Is he your main suspect now?"

"I saw him in front of Graham's office and followed him. He led me to his hotel. I talked to a clerk, and a whore there, and they both described Lillian Graham as having visited him there. On more than one occasion."

"I see."

"If they're . . . involved, it makes sense to me that they planned the doctor's death, and Rufus is the one who did it. After all, he was beaten to death."

"And that's pretty much Rufus Holmes's trademark," Boone said. "I don't even think he carries a weapon."

"What do you think the sheriff will think?"

"He's still kind of sold on the lady doctor, but he'll listen. He's a reasonable man."

"Is he getting any pressure?"

"Pressure?"

"You know what I mean."

"Political pressure?"

Clint nodded.

"Well, he has been talkin' to the mayor," Boone said. "The town council would like a quick ending to the matter."

"That figures."

"But he won't arrest the lady doctor just to make them happy," Boone said. "He won't make an arrest without evidence."

"Well then," Clint said, "I guess I'll just have to find him some."

TWENTY-TWO

They had another beer each before leaving the saloon. Clint made note of the place's location, and the name: Tom's Tavern.

"Tavern," Clint said as they left. "That's a British term, isn't it?"

"I don't know," Boone said. "Never been out of North America myself."

When they reached the sheriff's office, the man had still not returned.

"I reckon I'll have to go and look for him," Boone said. "Where will you be?"

"My hotel, I guess, or the doctor's office."

"Okay," Boone said. "When I find him, we'll come and see you."

"All right."

"You can make your case to Sheriff Brown and we'll see what he says."

Clint shook hands with the man and left the office.

* * *

He went back to the doctor's office, found both Lissa Sugarman and Marietta hard at work.

"I thought you were going to take a rest," Clint said to the doctor.

"I will," she said. "I just need to give Marietta a few more instructions."

"Where is she?"

"In with the patients. Do you want to come in?"

"Sure."

"Come."

Clint followed Lissa into the other room. It looked a lot like a bunkhouse, with beds fitted in at every angle.

"Was this supposed to be his hospital?" Clint asked.

"The beginning of one, I guess," she said.

Marietta straightened up from the patient she had been tending to.

"Dr. Graham was a great man," she said. "He was going to give Veracruz a real hospital."

"Not if his wife could help it," Clint said.

"You know?" Marietta asked, eyes wide.

"Know what?"

"That one," she said, "the doctor's wife. She is an evil woman."

"Well," Clint said, "I know she's a hard woman."

"What do you mean by *evil*, Marietta?" Dr. Sugarman asked.

"He hated her, and she hated him," Marietta said, "but even though he was a great man, Dr. Graham was weak. And she was strong—very strong."

"She dominated him."

"Yes," Marietta said. "She did not want him to help people. She was very . . . greedy."

"How did she expect him to make money if he didn't help people?" Lissa asked.

Marietta shrugged.

"I only know she did not want him to spend money building a hospital."

"Well," Clint said, "she has her way now."

"What will happen to the hospital?" Marietta asked. "What will happen here?"

"I imagine after these patients are sent home, she'll close this place down," Clint said.

"B-But now we have another doctor," Marietta said.

"I'll have to go back to my own office, Marietta," Lissa said.

The young Mexican girl looked at her.

"Will I be able to work for you?"

"I—I don't know," Lissa said. "I wouldn't be able to pay you much."

"That does not matter," the girl said. "At least . . . I wouldn't have to be . . . be home."

"I'm sure your husband wants you home, Marietta," Clint said.

"He is not my husband," she said. "He was married to my mother."

"I see," Clint said.

"I do not want to go back there," she said. "He is . . . cruel."

"Cruel," Clint said, looking at Lissa. "Seems to be a lot of that going around."

Lissa went to Marietta and put her arms around the girl's shoulders.

"Don't worry," she said. "I'll need you here for a while. You can stay here."

"But what will happen after she closes this place?" Marietta asked.

"I don't know," Lissa said. "Why don't we just take care of things here and we'll deal with it later."

"Doctor?" Clint cut in. "Can I talk to you for a minute?"

"Of course." Lissa patted Marietta's shoulder. "Take care of the patients. I'll be right back."

"Yes, Doctor."

They went back into the office.

"Do you have a gun?" he asked.

"I—I don't, but the doctor may have had one around here someplace."

"Let's take a look."

It didn't take long for them to determine that there was no gun on the premises—or so they thought.

"Señor Adams?"

They turned and saw Marietta standing in the doorway.

"Yes?" Clint said. "What is it, Marietta?"

"I have this," she said, and brought a Navy Colt out from beneath her skirts.

"Jesus," Clint said, "that might blow up in your hand."

He went to her and took the gun.

"Where did you get this?"

"I took it from . . . from home."

He checked it over, found that it was in good working order.

"Will it work?" Lissa asked.

"Oh yeah, it'll work fine." He turned to Lissa. "Can you shoot?"

"I—I never have," she said.

Clint looked at Marietta.

"I can shoot, señor," she said.

"Then I guess you better hold on to this."

He handed her the gun back. She took it into the other room with her.

"Why do we need a gun?" Lissa asked Clint.

"I think the doctor's wife had him killed," Clint said. "And I wouldn't put it past her to try to kill you, too."

"Oh, my . . ."

"Lissa, you could leave here if you wanted to," he said. "Nobody would blame you."

"I can't do that, Clint," she said. "Who would take care of these people?"

"All right, then," he said. "There's a man, a big, dark-haired man named Rufus. I think he and Mrs. Graham killed the doc. So if he comes walking through this door, you shoot him—or have Marietta shoot him. Understand?"

"I understand."

He gave her a better, more accurate description of Rufus Holmes.

"Got it?" he asked.

"I've got it," she said. "I only hope Marietta *can* shoot."

"I'll bring another gun back with me later," he said. "And I'll show you how to use it."

"All right," she said. "All right, that would be . . . better."

TWENTY-THREE

Clint went back to his hotel to retrieve his little Colt New Line. The .32-caliber revolver would be easier for Lissa Sugarman or Marietta to handle than that big Navy Colt. He tucked the gun into his belt, at the small of his back.

He returned to the lobby and was about to leave when Sheriff Brown came walking in.

"Just the man I've been lookin' for," Brown said.

"Likewise, Sheriff."

"Yeah, Boone told me you were tryin' to find me," Brown said. "I had some trouble in one of the saloons I had to take care of."

"Boone tell you why I wanted you?"

"He did," Brown said. "I'm not sure I agree with you, Adams, but it's somethin' to look into. I figure to go and talk to Mrs. Graham, and to Rufus Holmes."

"You know Holmes?"

"I've had him in my cells a time or two, but never for anythin' big I could prove. Can't say I can see him and Mrs. Graham as a couple, though."

"A man could do a lot of things for money, Sheriff."

"That's true enough. Where are you headed?"

"Back to the doctor's office. Got two women there need looking after."

"You thinkin' they're in danger from Mrs. Graham or Rufus?"

"Or both," Clint said. "She doesn't like Lissa Sugarman very much, and she already fired Marietta once, just for being pretty."

"Marietta?" Brown asked. "Doc Graham's nurse?"

"Yeah, I went and found her and gave her back her job, for a while anyway."

"How did Manolo take that?" Brown asked. "Pretty happy, I bet."

"Manolo? The big fat fella she lives with? I thought he was her husband."

"Ain't hardly," Brown said, "although he treats her like a wife—a Mexican wife."

"She doesn't want to go back to him."

"She don't have to if she don't want to," Brown said, "but if I was you, I wouldn't get in the middle."

"I'll leave that for later," Clint said. "If you're going to talk to Rufus Holmes, I'd like to come along."

"Boone told me you won't wear a badge," Brown said. "It would make it easier to have you along if you would."

"He told me you've been talking to your mayor."

"The mayor wants me to find out who killed Dr. Graham, and he wants it done quick."

"Does he want you to find out who really did it," Clint asked, "or does he want you to pin it on somebody quick?"

"I don't think he cares," Brown said, "but I do. I want the bastard who actually did it."

"You'd probably find that out faster if you forgot about Dr. Sugarman as a suspect."

"We'll see," Brown said. "Right now I'll go back to the doctor's office with you. After that, Mrs. Graham, and then Rufus."

"Okay, Sheriff," Clint said. "You call the shots."

"Thank you, Mr. Adams."

"Clint, just call me Clint."

"Okay, Clint," the sheriff said. "Let's go. Your two ladies are waitin'."

When they reached Dr. Graham's office, they heard screaming from upstairs. It was a woman, and she sounded pretty angry. When they entered, they saw Lillian Graham standing there, yelling at both Lissa and Marietta.

". . . don't belong in here, and I want you two bitches out of here now!" she was screaming.

Marietta looked frightened, but Lissa just looked exhausted.

"Mrs. Graham," she said, "somebody needs to look after these people."

"Not you," Lillian said, "so you get your skinny little ass out of here."

"Not until these people are cared for." Then Lissa saw the sheriff and Clint. "I'll stay as long as the sheriff wants me to."

"Thank you, Doctor," Sheriff Brown said.

Lillian whirled on him, and her face was a mask of hatred and rage.

"You! You put this bitch in here?"

"Like she said, Mrs. Graham, somebody needed to care for these people."

"This was my husband's property," Lillian said, "and now it's mine. I want you all out, and if you're so worried about those patients, take them, too."

"Mrs. Graham," the sheriff said, "I think you should come with me."

"Where?"

"Someplace I think we'll be able to straighten this all out—jail."

TWENTY-FOUR

As they entered the sheriff's office, Lillian Graham asked, "Am I under arrest?"

"For what?" Brown asked.

"For murdering my husband, of course. Are you a dense man, Sheriff?"

"Mrs. Graham, if you were under arrest for killing anyone, you'd be in chains. Sit down."

She ignored him.

"If I am not under arrest, what am I doing here?"

"You're here for questioning."

"About what?"

"Well now, that would be your husband's murder."

"You asked me about that already," she said impatiently.

"I know," the sheriff said. "It's Mr. Adams, here, who has some questions."

She turned and looked at Clint, then back at Sheriff Brown.

"He is not a lawman. Besides, I already spoke with him as well."

"He's got some new questions."

She glared at the lawman, then turned, looked at Clint, and folded her arms.

"You know a man named Rufus Holmes?"

If he expected her to be shocked, he was disappointed.

"Rufus? Is that what this is about?"

"So you do know him?"

"Of course," she said. "He fucks me, brutalizes me in a way my husband could never have imagined. And I love it. Anything else?"

Clint looked at Sheriff Brown, who was red-faced and shocked.

"You're not going to shock me, Mrs. Graham, so stop trying," Clint said. "You're only scandalizing the sheriff."

Now it was Brown giving him a dirty look, not Lillian Graham.

"You think I had Rufus kill my husband," she said.

"The thought had crossed my mind."

"Well, it wouldn't surprise me if Rufus did it," she said, "but if he did, I didn't know anything about it. So I guess that means you're going to have to talk to him."

"I plan to," Clint said.

"So do I," Brown said, recovered now. "Mrs. Graham, I want you to stay away from your husband's practice while Dr. Sugarman is there."

"What?" She whirled on the lawman. "I own that building—"

"Not until after you husband's will is read," Clint said. "I assume he had a will?"

"Well, yes—"

"And usually the will is read after the funeral," Clint said. "When is the funeral?"

"I—I don't know," she said. "His body is still at the undertaker's." She turned to Brown. "When can I bury him?"

"Not until I find out who killed him."

"What?" she asked again.

"And since his will won't be read until after," Clint said, "I guess you don't own that building yet—if, indeed, he even left it to you."

"You can't do this!" she said.

"I'm doin' it," Brown said. "Those people need to be treated, and Dr. Sugarman is the only doctor in town."

"That's my building!" she shouted.

"Ma'am," Sheriff Brown said, "if I catch you in that building again, or anywhere near Dr. Sugarman or the nurse, Marietta, I'll toss you in a cell."

"You can't do that," she said. "I won't stand for it."

"That's right, you won't stand for it," Brown said. "You'll sit for it, in a cell. Mrs. Graham, go home and stay there."

"Wha—"

"I'd do as he says, before he puts you in a cell now," Clint advised.

He took her by the elbow, escorted her to the door, opened it, deposited her outside, and then closed it. Then he looked over at the sheriff, who had seated himself behind his desk.

"Think that'll do it?" the sheriff asked.

Clint walked back to the desk.

"It should," Clint said. "If that doesn't drive her to Rufus, nothing will."

"And you think she'll have Rufus kill someone else?"

"Yes."

"Who?"

"Well," Clint said, "you, me, Lissa, Marietta, one of us."

"That's the best you can do?"

"Sorry."

"Great."

TWENTY-FIVE

"Why would a woman want to be brutalized by a man?"

Clint turned his head and looked at Deputy Boone. He'd found Boone in his favorite saloon and the deputy offered to buy him a beer. While they drank, Clint told Boone about the meeting with Lillian Graham in the sheriff's office.

"Apparently," Clint said, "it's because her husband would never do it."

"Yeah, but . . . he was her husband. Maybe he didn't want to—although from everything I've heard, she sure deserved a smack or two."

Clint studied Boone.

"Deputy, are you . . . easily shocked?"

"At my age?" Boone asked. "Why do you ask?"

"Because Lillian managed to make the sheriff blush with her comments."

"She did?"

"Yeah."

"Well, the sheriff is kind of a prude about women."

Clint stared at Boone.

"What? Isn't that the word? Prude?"

"At his age?"

"He doesn't have much experience with women."

"Okay," Clint said, "listen, the sheriff said I could use you to watch Lissa and Marietta."

"The lady doctor and the little Mexican nurse?" Boone asked.

"Yeah."

"You want me to guard them?"

"Right."

"Why not use the kid, Ed?"

"Would you trust the lives of two women to an inexperienced deputy?"

"Uh, no."

"Then you'll do it?"

"It's not an order from the cap'n?"

"No, it's not an order, Deputy," Clint said. "I'm asking as a favor."

"A favor to you, or the cap'n?"

"Does it make a difference?"

"Yeah," Boone said. "See, the cap'n owes me a favor. It's his turn."

"I see. Well, this one's a favor for me."

"Okay."

"Okay, what?"

"I'll do it."

"Oh. Thanks."

"Just tell me one thing."

"What's that?"

"Who am I protecting them from?"

"Rufus Holmes."

Boone nodded and said, "I'm gonna need a bigger gun."

TWENTY-SIX

After Deputy Boone got himself a bigger gun—a shotgun, in fact—Clint walked Boone over to the doctor's office and introduced him to Lissa Sugarman and Marietta.

"The deputy is going to stay here with you, just in case," Clint said.

"In case of what?" Lissa asked.

"Well . . . in case Lillian Graham comes back," Clint said. "The sheriff has warned her to stay away from here until all the patients are gone."

"Will she?"

"I don't know."

"What if she does not?" Marietta asked. She was standing in the doorway to the next room. "Will he shoot her?"

"No, ma'am," Boone said, "but I will arrest her."

"So why the shotgun?" Lissa asked.

Deputy Boone shrugged and said, "Well, you just never know, ma'am."

*　*　*

Marietta went into the other room to be with the patients. Clint took Lissa by the elbow and pulled her aside.

"Bone is here in case Lillian tries something," he said, "or sends someone."

"And what will you be doing?" she asked.

"I'm going to continue to try and find out exactly who killed Dr. Graham."

"And how will you do that?"

"By asking questions of people who know both Lillian and Rufus Holmes."

"Is that her . . . man?"

"Yes," Clint said, "her lover."

"What would this man see in her?" she asked. "I mean, I'm not being cruel but—"

"I know what you mean," Clint said, "but you might not ask that if you saw Rufus—and I hope you never do."

"Will you come back?" she asked.

"In the morning," Clint said. "Are you and Marietta sleeping here?"

"Yes," Lissa said, "she doesn't want to go home."

"All right," Clint said. "Deputy Boone will be here all night. I'm going back to my hotel, but I'll check here in the morning. Meanwhile, here."

He took out the Colt New Line and handed it to her.

"Just hold it like this, cock it, hold it steady, and pull the trigger. Aim for the largest part of your target, which would be the upper part of the body. And if it's Rufus Holmes, it'll be a large target."

"How many times do I pull the trigger?"

"Until the gun is empty, and the hammer is falling on empty chambers."

"A-All right."

She was wearing a smocklike dress that had large pockets on the sides.

"Keep the gun in your pocket," he said. "Don't put it down anywhere."

"I have to admit y-you're frightening me."

"Good," Clint said, "you should be frightened. But also remember you can leave anytime you want. You're basically a volunteer here. Nobody will stop you from walking out."

"No," she said, "these people need me. I have to stay."

"I admire you for that," he said. "And I'll do my best to make sure you and Marietta are safe."

"I'm afraid our little nurse may have a crush on you, Clint," Lissa said.

"Really? And how about our doctor?"

"Well . . ." She blushed. "I think I better check on my patients."

"I'll see you in the morning, then."

"Yes," she said, still uncomfortable. "Good night."

"Good night, Lissa."

Clint went over to Deputy Boone, who had taken up a position in a wooden chair by the front door.

"I'll be back in the morning. You need anything?" Clint asked.

"Yeah," Boone said. "This chair is real uncomfortable."

"You want me to get you a pillow?"

"No," Boone said, "I want you to get whatever you're doin' done . . . quick."

"I'll do my best, Deputy."

"And what's the sheriff gonna be doin' all this time?" Boone asked.

"Same as me," Clint said. "Trying to find the evidence on whoever killed Dr. Graham."

TWENTY-SEVEN

It was too early to turn in, and Clint knew that Josephina kept her cantina open later for people with late appetites. "Drunk hombres are hungry hombres," she had told him.

It seemed to be the truth, for as he approached the front door of her place, three drunken Mexicans were leaving—although they were probably less drunk than they had been when they entered, since they had now eaten.

As he entered, he saw that the place was empty. Josephina came out of the kitchen, wiping her hands on her apron.

"Well, well," she said, "there you are. Have you found another place to eat?"

"There is no other place to eat in this town," he assured her.

"What about another bed to sleep in?"

"I've been sleeping in my own bed, Josephina," he said. "Honest."

"Sí, but with who?"

"Now, now," Clint said, "here I've been busy trying to solve a murder, and you accuse me of sleeping with someone else?"

"Well, I have not heard from you since I came to your room," she said. "Don't tell me you have still been waitin' for me to come to you again?"

"No," he said, "I've just been very busy, and now I'm very hungry."

"Hmph," she said, crossing her arms beneath her big breasts, almost pushing them up and out of her peasant blouse. "So now you want me to feed you."

"Yes," he said, "please."

She sighed and said, "Very well. Sit down. I think I still have some food left."

She had plenty of food left and brought him platters full. She sat with him while he ate.

"So who has been murdered—oh wait, you are talkin' about the gringo doctor?"

"Yes."

"Madre de Dios," she said. "That was terrible. Who would beat to death el médico?"

"That's what I'm trying to find out."

While he ate, he explained to her how Dr. Sugarman and the nurse, Marietta, had been caring for Dr. Graham's patients since his death.

"The doctora, she is beautiful, no?" Josephina asked.

"Have you seen her?" Clint asked, wondering if he could get away with a lie.

"Oh, sí," Josephina said, "I went to her one day when I burned my hand."

"Then yes," he said, "she is very beautiful."

"More beautiful than I am?" she asked, sitting up straight.

"Different," Clint said. "You are both very beautiful."

She punched him on the arm.

"You wanted me to tell the truth, didn't you?" he asked.

"No," she said, "I wanted you to tell me I am the most beautiful."

"Well," Clint said, "while you're both beautiful, you are the one who can cook."

She folded her arms and glared at him, still not happy.

"And you're the one," he added, "who will be coming to my room tonight."

"Because you are inviting me?" she asked.

"Yes," he said with a smile, "I'm inviting you."

TWENTY-EIGHT

Rufus Holmes had moved out of his hotel and into the big house with Lillian Graham. He woke up that morning with weak legs. That woman was insatiable, had kept him up most of the night having sex, and that meant that she took a lot of punishment. He'd never seen a woman who liked punishment so much.

She came into the room now, wearing a dressing gown, and he said, "Again?"

"No, not again," she said. "My ass is sore enough . . . for a while. Come downstairs. Breakfast is ready, and we have to talk."

"I'll be right there."

She left the room and he got dressed. Maybe he'd finally worn her out, for a change. As he went downstairs, he could smell the bacon and coffee. Maybe this wouldn't be a bad life, for a while.

As he entered the dining room, she was putting breakfast on the table.

"No servants?"

"I don't want to make it obvious yet that you're here," she told him. "Sit."

He sat, piled his plate with eggs, bacon, biscuits. By God, the woman could cook?

"Enjoying it?" she asked, seated across from him.

"Oh, yeah."

"And the sex?"

"Well . . . yeah, you know that."

"And the money," she said, "you're going to enjoy the money."

With his mouth full, he asked, "What's your point?"

"If we want to keep living this life, certain things have to be done," she said.

"Like what?"

"Like murder," she said.

He stared at her.

"I thought that was how we got here?" he asked.

"Yes," she said, "but if we want to stay here—if you want to stay here—then more people have to die."

He took a big mouthful of coffee and swallowed thoughtfully.

"Who?" he asked finally.

Clint woke with Josephine's head on his chest, her breasts pressed to him. He put his arms around her, held her that way for a few moments, his face in her hair. It smelled like her cooking. Then he ran his hands down her bare back, enjoying the feel of her smooth skin. One hand came to rest at the small of her back and she stirred. She lifted her head, looked at him, then kissed him. He kissed her back. She slid one leg over him and straddled him. His penis swelled between them. She rubbed her hairy thatch up and down him, wetting him with her juices before actually taking him inside her.

She leaned over him so her big breasts dangled in his face. He reached for them, held them, squeezed them, sucked on those amazing nipples while she rode him, her hair a wild black cloud around her head.

She rode him that way for a while, her hips never stopping. He let her have her way for a long time, but finally flipped her onto her back so abruptly that she yelled—but didn't object.

He hooked his elbows underneath her knees, spread her wide, and pounded into her without stopping until they both finished with a long groan from him and a loud shout from her . . .

"Breakfast?" he asked.

"Soon," she said, her head on his shoulder. "First I need to rest."

"No," he said, "I don't mean I want you to cook it. There must be someplace else in this town that has decent food. I'll take you out for breakfast."

She lifted her head and stared at him.

"Really?"

"Why not?"

"I have not been to a restaurant in Veracruz in . . . well, a very long time."

"Well, let's make today the day."

"But . . . I need some clean clothes."

"You'll look fine—"

"Cabrón!" she snapped, slapping him on the chest. "I cannot go somewhere to eat wearin' the same clothes I wore yesterday!"

"Okay, okay," he said. "We'll stop by your rooms and you can get some fresh clothes."

She sat up in bed, pulling the sheet up to her neck, and said, "And now I must decide where to eat."

TWENTY-NINE

Clint expected Josephina to take him to some fancy restaurant in a better part of town, maybe one that she'd been
wanting to eat in for a long time. Instead, they only went a
few blocks from her place, where most of the customers
seemed to be dockworkers and sailors, with a few other
citizens sprinkled among them.

Fish was never a favorite meal of Clint's. He usually
only ate it when it was all he could get, when he was on
the trail and camped near a stream. Since Veracruz was
right on the water, fish was popular, and Josephina said
she was taking him for some of the best fish she'd ever
tasted.

As they entered, an older black woman came rushing
up to them, took Josephina's hands in her worked-hardened
ones.

"Josephina, my girl," she said. "This is unexpected. Why,
child, you haven't eaten with us in so long."

"I cannot afford your prices, Auntie," Josephina said.

"Well, you know you can eat here anytime you want," the woman said.

"I know that, but I would hate for people to come to my cantina for free food."

"The truth is," Auntie said, looking at Clint, "I would feed her for free, me, and she would feed me for free, and that is why we do not feed each other."

"This is my new amigo, Clint Adams," Josephina said. "He wanted to take me out to eat, and I told him there was only one place in town I wanted to go."

"I'm honored to have you both. Please, come." There was only the merest flicker on Auntie's face, but Clint knew she had recognized his name.

She showed them to a table, promised to return with coffee.

"She's not Mexican, and she's your aunt?" he asked.

"She's everybody's aunt," Josephina said.

"There's no name outside," he said. "What is it—oh, wait."

Josephina smiled and said, "Yes, she calls her restaurant 'Auntie's.'"

The woman returned with coffee and asked them what they wanted to eat.

"Well," Clint said, "I'm not used to having fish for breakfast."

"I can cook you what you want, me," the woman said. "But if you would permit me, I'll prepare something special that I think you will like."

Clint sipped the coffee, found it just the way he liked it, which was encouragement enough.

"All right," he said. "I'm in your hands."

"Josephina?"

"I, too, am in your hands, Auntie."

Auntie clapped her hands happily and went to her kitchen. There were two waitresses working the floor, as Auntie's was roughly three times the size of Josephina's place. But it was Auntie, herself, who would wait on them, and the other waitresses stayed away.

When Auntie returned with two plates, she set them down in front of the two younger people proudly. Josephina clapped her hands.

"Auntie's poached eggs and salmon," she said happily.

"With bacon," Auntie said. "Please, enjoy. I will bring some biscuits."

There was already bread beneath the eggs and salmon, but Clint did not refuse the biscuits.

"Try it," Josephina said anxiously.

Clint cut into his breakfast and took a forkful into his mouth.

"Wow," he said truthfully, "that's great. But the bread . . ."

"It's corn bread," Josephina said. "Auntie's own recipe."

They were both eating avidly by the time Auntie returned with a basket of biscuits, which made her very happy.

"I'll bring more coffee."

As she went back to the kitchen, Clint asked, "Where's she from?"

"New Orleans."

"I knew I heard a Cajun accent there. How did she come to be here?"

"I do not know," Josephina said. "I believe she came here to escape a bad affair of the heart."

"How long has she been here?"

"As long as I can remember," Josephina said.

"This is wonderful," Clint said. "This is . . . almost as good as your cooking."

"You are very sweet," she said, "but if I could cook as wonderfully as Auntie, I would leave here and open a restaurant in . . . San Francisco."

Auntie returned with more coffee, poured their mugs full, and then gazed at them happily.

"This one," she said to Clint, touching Josephina's head, "is my favorite. If you hurt her, I will poison you, me."

"If you poisoned me with food this good," Clint said, "I'd probably still eat it."

Auntie looked at Josephina.

"This one knows how to talk, eh?"

"Yes, Auntie," she said, "he does."

"I will leave you to enjoy your breakfast," the older woman said. She looked at Clint. "If you want more, you just say so."

"Yes, Auntie."

Clint stared at the woman's face and suddenly became aware that she was much older than she seemed. As she hurried back to her kitchen, she moved with no sign of age.

"How old is she?" Clint asked.

"I have never asked."

"She could be . . . sixty, or eighty."

"Eighty, I think," Josephina said.

"But she moves so young."

"She eats her own food," Josephina said.

"I suppose that's it," Clint said. "I think this breakfast is going to put an extra spring in my step, at that."

"Thank you for bringing me here," Josephina said. "It has been a long time since I ate Auntie's cooking."

"I should thank you, Josephina," Clint said. "Even when you're not cooking for me yourself, you're keeping me well fed."

For the remainder of the meal they kept silent and just ate.

THIRTY

Rufus Holmes knew where to go to recruit men for the jobs he needed done. And with Lillian Graham's money behind him, he knew he'd be able to hire the best.

He went directly to the docks. He could have grabbed half a dozen dockworkers or sailors off the docks cheap, but Rufus Holmes was not going cheap anymore.

Not ever.

He started across the street to Auntie's restaurant, then stopped short when he saw Clint Adams coming out with a Mexican girl. He had seen Adams at the Graham house only briefly, from hiding, but he knew him when he saw him. He knew Adams was the Gunsmith, but that didn't matter much. With enough money he could hire enough men to take care of even the Gunsmith.

He backed up, stepped behind a buckboard that was standing in the street, and crouched down. The men he wanted would be eating in Auntie's, but he'd never expected to find Adams eating there as well. He waited to

see which way Clint and the woman would walk when
they left, but before they could leave, Auntie herself grabbed
them. Rufus waited . . .

"You make sure you bring your friend back," Auntie told
Josephina, then turned to Clint and said, "and you make
sure my girl comes back to see me."

"I will, Auntie," Clint said.

"I take that as a promise, me."

"I'll remember," Clint said.

As they left Auntie's and started down the street,
Josephina said, "She will keep you to your promise,
you know."

"I'll just have to bring you back here at least once, before I leave town."

"And when will you be leaving?"

"Not for a few days, at least," he told her.

"Good," she said, "because once you leave, I do not
think I will eat at Auntie's again for a long time."

"It's kind of silly that neither of you eats the other's
cooking," he said. "Does she like your cooking?"

"She loves Mexican food, and loves my cooking."

"Seems to me the solution would be to go into business
together," Clint said. "That way you can cook for the pub-
lic, and for each other."

Josephina looked at him funny, then fell silent as he
walked her home.

Rufus watched as Clint Adams walked away with the
Mexican girl he thought looked like Josephina, who owned

her own cantina. He waited until they were out of sight, then crossed the street to Auntie's.

"Rufus!" she yelled as he entered. "Where you been, you? When you don't eat here, my business goes down."

"Hello, Auntie."

Rufus knew a lot of hard men from the docks, and they all loved Auntie. This woman did not have any enemies that he knew of. It was amazing to him that someone could be liked by everybody—including him.

"I'm lookin' for Franco. Have you seen him today?"

"Not yet," she said, "but he eats here five days a week, and so far he only been here four."

Franco Colon was death for hire. Rufus enjoyed hurting people, but when you needed someone killed, you looked for Franco. They had worked together many times before, but even though they were friends, Franco was the only man Rufus Holmes was afraid of. He could kill with a knife, a gun, or his hands.

And he had other friends.

"If you see Franco," he told Auntie, "let him know that I'm lookin' for him. I got work for him."

"I don't want to hear about your business," she said, shaking her head, "but I tell him if I see him."

"Tell him if he sits still for at least an hour, I'll find him," Rufus said. "Tell him that."

"I tell him, but that boy, he don't sit still for long."

Franco knew he had a lot of enemies, and sitting still would make him a target.

"I'll find 'im," he told Auntie. "Just give him the message."

"I'll give it to him. You gonna stay and eat?"

"Not today, Auntie," he said, "but soon."

"Yeah, soon," she said, "if I don't go out of business, me."

"Auntie," he said, "you ain't never goin' out of business. Not the way you cook."

"You better be right," she told him, "or I'm gonna blame you."

"Don't worry," he said, "I just need a few days to handle some business, and I'll be eatin' here."

"You be careful, Rufus," she said.

"I'm always careful, Auntie."

THIRTY-ONE

Clint walked Josephina back to her place, where she had to prepare to open for business that day. He promised to see her later.

"What are you going to be doing today, hombre?" she asked.

"Like I told you," he said, "I've got to find out who killed the doctor."

"So you are going to see your lady doctor, eh?" She gave him a stern look.

"She's not my lady doctor," Clint said, "but yes, I have to go and check on her."

"Well, you just remember what last night was like with Josephina when you see her," she said. "You think of me, eh?"

"I'll be thinking of you all day, but you think about . . . this," he said, kissing her soundly and then releasing her.

"Cabrón!" she said, pushing him away.

"I'll see you later."

He started away, then turned while she was unlocking her door.

"Clint?" she asked. "Is something wrong?"

"Josephina, tell me something."

"Sí?"

"Do you know a man named Rufus?"

"A big gringo, who likes to hurt people," she said. "Sí, I know him."

"Well?"

"I know him when I see him," she said, "but I do not *know* him. Comprendes?"

"I understand," he said. "So what *do* you know about him?"

"Just what I said. He likes to hurt people, and he is paid to do it."

"What about murder?"

"I don't understand," she said, looking puzzled. "What about it?"

"Have you heard any word that he does murder for hire?"

"No," she said, very definite about it. "I have never heard about him killing people. Hurt, yes, but kill, no."

"And how well do you know what goes on down on the docks?"

"I know what I hear," she said, shrugging, eyeing him curiously. "Why?"

"If you were going to have somebody killed," he said, "who would you hire?"

"A man or a woman?" she asked.

"Does it matter?"

"Who and why matter to me, hombre. If it was a man

who cheated on me, or a puta who stole my man, I would want to kill them myself."

"Okay, but let's just say you don't want to do it yourself. Who would you hire?"

"There is only name I can think of," she said. "The thing he enjoys the most is killing. Rufus, he likes to hurt people, but . . ."

"What's his name?"

She turned, looked at him, and said, "You must be very careful of this man. He is not like Rufus. He does not kill for pleasure. It is his business, and he is very good at it."

"I'm always careful, Josephina," he said. "What's the name?"

She sighed and said, "Franco."

THIRTY-TWO

When Clint arrived at the doctor's office, he could see the relief on both Lissa and Marietta's faces.

"Are you all right?" he asked Lissa.

"Yes, yes," she said, "just glad to see you. With you here, I know I won't have to shoot anyone."

"What about Boone?"

"He's fine," she said. "He doesn't talk very much, though."

"That's okay," Clint said, "he's not here to talk. He's here to protect you."

"Doctor?" Marietta called from the doorway. "Buenos días, Clint."

"Good morning, Marietta."

"Coming, Marietta," Lissa said. She touched Clint's arm and followed Marietta into the other room. Clint took the opportunity to talk to Boone.

"Boone, you want to go and get some breakfast?" he asked.

"The ladies and me went out and ate," Boone said. "But thanks."

"Well, if you want to go home for a few hours—"

"I got nothin' goin' on at home, Clint," Boone said. "I'll just stay."

"Okay," Clint said. "Listen, what do you know about a man named Franco?"

"Franco?" Boone asked, surprised. "How'd you hear about him?"

"I asked who the murder for hire man was in town and got his name."

"Well, yeah, he does murder for hire—or that's what we hear. We've never caught him in the act, which is about the only way we'd be able to get him. Why are you getting' mixed up with him? You have enough trouble with Rufus Holmes."

"Yeah, but I heard that Rufus Holmes is not a killer," Clint said, "and we're looking for a killer."

"So you pick Franco?"

"If Lillian Graham goes to Rufus and wants someone killed, who would Rufus go to?"

Boone paused, then shrugged and said, "Probably Franco. We know they've worked together."

"Okay," Clint said, "I better go and talk to the sheriff."

"What are you gonna do?"

"I'm not sure," Clint said. "I did have plans just to ask more questions, but maybe we should go and find Franco and have a talk."

"You think the sheriff is gonna go with you?" Boone asked.

"I don't know him that well," Clint said. "Do you?"

Boone thought a moment before speaking.

"The sheriff don't like to push," Boone said. "You do. It'll be interesting."

"Would you rather I wait so that Rufus and Franco come here together?"

"Hey," Boone said, raising his shotgun, "I got two barrels."

Clint liked that Boone didn't scare.

"I'll talk to the sheriff and let you know what happens."

"Like I said," Boone replied. "Interesting."

"I'll say good-bye to the ladies before I leave," Clint said.

"By the way," Boone said, "are you and the lady doctor . . . ?"

"No," Clint said. "Why, you interested?"

"No," Boone said, "curious. My days with the ladies are over. It's just me and my shotgun now."

"I hope you're very happy."

Boone grinned, rubbed the shotgun's barrel, and said, "Oh, we are."

Clint went to the doorway of the other room, watched Lissa and Marietta moving around the beds. Lissa stopped to lean over the little girl, touch her face, and smile.

"How's she doing?" Clint asked when Lissa came over to him.

"She's doing well," Lissa said, "and so am I. I saved the leg."

"You must be a hell of a doctor," Clint said. "First my foot, then her leg."

"Oh yes," Lissa said, "you were definitely in danger of losing that foot."

"I have to go," he said. "I'll be back later. By the way, I think the deputy might be interested in you—if you can woo him away from his shotgun."

She smiled and said, "Well, I'll have to keep that in mind."

THIRTY-THREE

Clint went to the sheriff's office and found the man there, apparently brooding over a cup of coffee.

"Problems?" he asked.

"I had to let the kid go."

"Wasn't working out?"

"The badge went to his head," Brown said.

"That happens."

"Get yerself a cup."

Clint went to the stove, poured himself a cup of coffee, then sat opposite the sheriff.

"What's on your mind?" the lawman asked.

"A man named Franco."

"A bad man," Brown said. "Boone was after him when he was sheriff, and I've been after him since I got to wear the star. What's your interest in him?"

"His specialty is murder."

"I thought you were figurin' on Rufus doin' that for the widow?"

"I'm getting' the word that Rufus doesn't kill," Clint said.

"Anybody kills," Brown said.

"So you don't believe it?" Clint asked. "You think he hires out for murder?"

Brown shrugged.

"Well, when I asked who does hire out, Franco was the name I got. And Boone says Franco and Rufus have worked together."

"He's right, they have. But that don't mean they are this time."

"Well, I'd like to ask him."

"Rufus? Go ahead, I ain't stoppin' you."

"Not Rufus. Franco."

"How do you intend to do that?"

"Find him, and ask him," Clint said. "I was hoping you'd help me with the first part."

"To find him, you'd have to go down to the docks," Brown said. "You want me to go with you? You know what kind of target I'd be with this tin on my chest?"

"Take it off."

"They'd still know who I am."

"Fine," Clint said. "Don't come with me. Just tell me where to look."

Brown gave it some thought.

"If you want to find anybody on the docks, there's only one person to ask."

"Who's that?"

"She has a business down there," Brown said.

"A woman?"

Brown nodded.

"They call her 'Auntie.'"

THIRTY-FOUR

When Clint entered Auntie's later that afternoon, most of the tables were empty. The woman's face betrayed surprise when he walked in.

"You came back already?" she asked. "My cookin' was that good, me?"

"Your cooking was excellent, Auntie," he said, "but that's not why I'm here. I want to talk."

"Talk?" she asked. "You want some chicory coffee while we talk?"

He didn't like anything mixed in with his coffee, but he said, "Sure."

"You go to that back table and wait," she said.

He walked to the table and sat down. Only two other tables were taken, one by a man, the other by a man and a woman, and they ignored him.

Auntie returned carrying a tray with a pot and two mugs. She sat and poured coffee for both of them, then stared at him across the table.

"So? What you want to talk about?"

"I'm told you know everybody on the docks," Clint said, "and that if I'm looking for someone, I should come here and ask you."

"That depends," Auntie said. "Who are you lookin' for?"

"A man named Franco," Clint said. "And another one named Rufus Holmes."

She sat back. "Whatchoo lookin' for them boys for?" she asked.

"I want to talk to them."

She laughed.

"Those boys don't talk."

"I know," Clint said. "One of them hurts people, and the other one kills them."

"One of them likes hurtin' people," she corrected. "That makes him real good at it. The other one kills for a livin'. If he don't kill, he don't eat, so when he gets a job, he gets it done."

"And do both of those boys eat here, Auntie?"

"They been known to," she said honestly.

"Uh-huh, and do you take messages for them?"

She squinted at him then smiled.

"Lots of people eat here," she said, "and once in a while they'll leave a message for each other."

"Now, I'm not asking you to betray any confidences, Auntie."

"That's good," she said, "'cause I don't do that. Some-body tells me somethin' in confidence, I take it to the grave, me."

Clint was starting to wonder if the Cajun accent was

put on for the benefit of others, so they wouldn't realize what a smart woman Auntie was.

"So you won't tell me where to find them, right?" Clint asked. "Like, if I wanted to hire them?"

"You don't want to hire them," she said. "You strike me as a man who does his own dirty work."

"You're right about that."

"And you got dirty work in mind for those boys."

"Only if they had something to do with the murder of Dr. Graham."

Her face became sad.

"That doctor, he was a good man," she said. "It wasn't right he was killed, and it wasn't right the way he was killed."

"I know."

"But you know what I think?" she asked.

"No, Auntie," he said, "I don't know what you think."

"I think maybe you lookin' in the wrong place," she said. "I think you lettin' certain reputations taint your thinkin'." She pointed a finger at him. "And you know about reputations, huh?"

He knew she'd recognized his name when they first met.

"I know," he said. "Are you telling me neither of them killed the doctor? And if you're telling me that, do you know who did?"

"I don't know nothin' about no murder," she said. "I'm just sayin' be careful how you think and where you look. These are rough boys, and even if they didn't kill that doctor, if they hear you're lookin' for them, you'll have to deal with them."

"Okay," he said, "I'll accept that. You pass the word that I'm looking for them."

"I can do that," she said, "but my girl, Josephina, gon' be real mad at me if I get you killed."

"Don't worry about that, Auntie," he said. "I'm not going to get killed."

"Uh-huh. Which of them boys you wanna see first? 'Cause you don't wanna see them together."

"Either way," Clint said. "I just want to see them. If they didn't have anything to do with killing the doctor, all they've got to do is tell me."

"Like I said," she told him, "those boys don't talk."

"Will you give them my message?"

She sat back and looked unconcerned.

"If they happen to come in here to eat," she said, "I guess I could mention somethin' about it."

THIRTY-FIVE

Rufus found Franco sitting at a back table in a small cantina filled with dockworkers. They all steered clear of the man, and did the same with Rufus as he crossed the room. It was the size of Rufus that deterred most men, but with Franco it was more than mere size. For one thing, he was not even six feet tall, but anyone who looked into his eyes knew they were looking at a killer. In point of fact, Franco was feared much more than Rufus was.

But Rufus had no problem approaching Franco. He was used to that dead-eye stare the other man gave everyone. He pulled out a chair and sat opposite the killer.

"Auntie told me you were lookin' for me," Franco said, his English only slightly accented. He had spent a lot of time north of the border, but he preferred the confines of his own country. "I do not like to stay in one place for too long, so speak quickly."

Rufus wanted to tell Franco to try that stare on someone else, but decided not to.

"I have a job for you," Rufus said.

"You have a job for me?" Franco asked with interest. "We usually do jobs together. Or you do your own alone. Why would you need to hire me?"

"It's not me," Rufus said, "it's my woman."

"The ugly gringa with all the money?" Franco asked. "The one with the dead doctor husband?"

"Yes."

"She has money?"

"Lots of money."

"And who does she want killed?"

"She wants a couple of people killed," Rufus said, "but one of them is Clint Adams."

"Clint Adams?" Now Franco was real interested. "You mean the Gunsmith?"

"Yeah."

"What is he doing in Veracruz?"

"Well, right now he's makin' my woman mad enough to want him killed."

"Who else?"

"The lady doctor who has taken over her husband's office."

"Is she taking care of his patients?"

"Yeah," Rufus said. "The sheriff asked her."

"Who will take care of them if I kill her?" Franco asked.

"Why does that matter?" the big man asked.

"It doesn't," Franco said, "but I am curious."

"She doesn't care," Rufus said. "Neither do I, and you shouldn't either."

"Will I be paid enough not to care?"

"You'll be paid plenty," Rufus said, "and any help you need will be paid, too."

"Help?"

"The woman has a deputy guarding her," Rufus said, "and there's a nurse."

"The lady doctor, she is the gringa, es verdad? The one they call 'Doc Veracruz'?"

"That's right."

"She does a lot of good down here on the docks," Franco said. "I will not be very popular if anyone finds out I killed her."

"Nobody will find out."

"And the nurse? Also a gringa?"

"No," Rufus said, "the nurse is a Mexican."

"I am to kill a Mexican girl? Why?"

"That's what the lady wants," Rufus said. "The girl was her husband's nurse and she fired her, now she's back."

Franco thought a moment, then said, "No, I will not kill her. She has done nothing."

"There is a lot of money—"

"You do it."

"What?"

"You kill the girl," Franco said, "I will kill the Gunsmith, and the gringa doctor."

"I don't—"

"You can keep the money for the girl," Franco said, "and you can have the girl to do what you want with first."

Rufus hesitated.

"Come on," Franco said, "you have been with this ugly gringa too long. What about a nice, pretty Mexican girl? She is pretty, no?"

"She is."

"Then you will do it?"

Rufus felt that Franco either didn't want to do it him-self, or he had some reason for wanting Rufus to do it. Maybe he wanted Rufus to be in it as deeply as he was.

And the little nurse was pretty. Rufus usually had to pay for pretty girls.

"All right," he said finally.

"You will do it?"

"I'll do it."

"Bueno," Franco said. "Then let us talk about money . . ."

THIRTY-SIX

Clint went from Auntie's to Josephina's. He needed a little more information about the Cajun lady.

"Hungry already?" Josephina asked as he entered. Her place was half full, and would continue to fill.

"I'm not here to eat, Josephina," he said. "Can I come into the kitchen?"

"Clint," she said, "I am busy. I do not have time for—" she started.

"It's not that," he said. "Besides, I wouldn't want to take a chance on either of us getting burned. I just want to ask you a few questions."

"All right," she said, "but I must keep working."

"That's fine," he said. "I'll try not to get in your way."

She took him into the kitchen, where there were pots and pans on the stove steaming and bubbling.

"What is it?" she asked.

"I want to know about Auntie."

"What about her?"

"Can I trust her?"

"To do what?"

Clint hesitated. Maybe Josephina didn't know that men like Rufus and Franco were also customers of Auntie's, acquaintances and, in some cases, maybe even friends. If Josephina was Auntie's "girl," maybe Rufus and Franco were two of her "boys."

"To deliver a message for me."

"A message?" Josephina repeated while stirring something in a pot. "Oh yes, she does that for many people."

"She does?"

Josephina nodded.

"She knows so many people that many come to her when they are looking for someone," Josephina said. "Auntie knows almost everyone in Veracruz."

"Did she know Dr. Graham and his wife?"

Josephina paused in her stirring.

"If she did, I am not aware," she said. "I should have said Auntie knows most of—how would you say it?—el común."

Clint thought a moment, then said, "Common?"

"Sí, yes," Josephina said, "the common people."

"So she didn't rub elbows with the wealthier people in town?"

Josephina laughed.

"No," she said, "Auntie lives and works down here with us, and also she is black *and* Cajun. There are not so many in the white community in Veracruz, and they do not come down here."

"Except for men like Rufus."

"Yes, Rufus," she said. "Men like him, for hire. How do you say—mercenario?"

"Mercenary," he said. "Mercenaries."

"Sí."

"And they eat at Auntie's?"

"Here, Auntie's," she said. "We both feed the sailors, the dockworkers, the laborers . . ."

"The common people."

"Sí."

"Josephina, do you also take messages and pass them on?"

"Sometimes."

"Like for Franco, if somebody's looking for him?"

"Sí."

"I asked Auntie to pass a message to him for me. Will she do it?"

"Yes, she will." She released the spoon she'd been using to stir and turned to face him. "But what message?"

"That I'm looking for him."

"When she tells him that—who you are and that you are lookin' for him—he will come to find you."

"That's what I want."

"And he will kill you."

"He'll try."

She grabbed his arm, took a fistful of his shirt.

"You must know that he will not come alone," she told him.

"I figure he'll bring Rufus, and some others."

"Ah," she said, releasing his shirt, "you are loco en la cabeza." She tapped her head to indicate she thought he was crazy in the head.

"That may be," he said, "but don't worry, I won't be alone either."

"I hope not," she said. She pointed her finger at him. "If you get killed, I will never forgive you."

"I'll keep that in mind."

"Now, get out," she said. "I have work."

"I'm going."

He turned, but she snapped, "Wait!"

He turned and she threw her arms around his neck and held on tightly, then released him.

"Now go!"

He left.

THIRTY-SEVEN

They chose a small saloon right on the docks. Franco decided he'd need four men. Rufus told him they'd have to pay them very little to make the money stretch.

"I thought your ugly gringa had much money."

"She will," he said, "after she buries her husband. Right now she's on kind of a budget."

"We will pay them little," Franco said, "but my friend, there will be much more for us after she buries him, eh?"

"Yes," Rufus said. But he thought, *Much more for me, maybe.*

They sat at a back table and interviewed the men as they came in. They were all muscle for hire, but Rufus and Franco were looking for men who would kill for a nickel. Many of those would come off the boats, looking for a quick dollar before they got back on and shipped out. They could commit murder and get away with it— and they also would not come back for more money.

Rufus sat with Franco but had no say while the Mexican chose his men. There were one or two men who Rufus knew and thought would be useful, but Franco disregarded them.

Rufus also noticed that Franco was not telling anyone about the Gunsmith—not yet anyway.

"Angel," Franco said to a tall, thin man who stepped up. "You are back?"

"For a day or two," Angel said. "Will that be enough time, amigo?"

"Plenty of time," Franco said. "Get yourself a drink, amigo."

Franco picked out four men, all Mexicans, had them go to the bar for a drink, and sent the rest home. It was getting dark out by the time he gathered the men at a table to tell them what they were in for.

"First," he said, "we have to kill a woman. Who has a problem with that?"

"A Mexican woman?" Angel asked.

Franco shook his head.

"A gringa doctor." He didn't tell them that Rufus would be killing a Mexican woman.

Angel shrugged, as did the others. No one had a problem with that.

"There might also be a deputy," Franco said.

"A Mexican deputy?" Angel asked.

"No," Franco said, "both the deputy and the sheriff are gringos."

"How can that be?" Angel asked.

Franco shrugged.

"I have no trouble killing lawmen," Angel said. The others agreed.

"Very well," Franco said, "then there is our main target."

"And who is that, amigo?" Angel asked.

"A gringo named Clint Adams."

There was silence and then one of the men said, "The Gunsmith?"

"That is right."

The men exchanged glances. None of them were gunmen. In fact, three of them killed with knives.

"I will kill the Gunsmith," Franco said, "with the aid of Angel. The rest of you will take care of the woman and the deputy."

The men seemed to heave a sigh of relief.

"Angel will be paid more for this reason," Franco said.

The other men didn't like that, until Franco said, "Any of you who wants to face the Gunsmith will be paid more as well. So?"

So . . . none of them volunteered.

"Very well," Franco said, "this is what will happen . . ."

Once the hired men were sent away, Franco and Rufus opened a bottle of whiskey.

"We do this tomorrow?" Franco said. "Will that satisfy your ugly gringa?"

"Would you stop saying that?"

"But she is ugly."

"I know it," Rufus said. "I don't have to be told every five minutes."

"How much longer will you stay with her?" Franco asked.

"Until this is over," Rufus said. "Until she buries her

husband and takes possession of the house and the money."

"Then what?"

"I don't want the house," Rufus said, "but I want that money."

"How will you take it from her?"

"Get her to go to the bank and take it out," Rufus said.

"And how will you convince her to do that?"

"I have this woman wrapped around . . . my finger," Rufus said. "Don't worry, I can do it."

"And then will you want to hire me to kill her?"

"I think," Rufus said, "that's one murder I'll be able to take care of myself."

They had a drink on it.

THIRTY-EIGHT

Clint went back to Dr. Graham's to let Deputy Boone, Lissa, and Marietta know that they could sleep peacefully that night.

"No one's going to come looking for us until at least tomorrow."

"How do you know that?" the deputy asked.

"I planted a seed today," Clint said. "I passed the word that I was looking for Rufus Holmes and his hired killer, who most likely is Franco."

"So how do you know they won't come tonight?" Lissa asked.

"They have to collect some more men," Clint said. "They won't come alone, and they won't come until they're sure I'm here as well. So that means that we have time."

"Time for what?" Boone asked.

"Time to move everybody out of here."

"Move them?" Lissa asked.

"Can they be moved without hurting them?" he asked.

"Well, yes . . . all but little Katrina."

"The girl with the injured leg?"

"That's right."

Clint frowned.

"No chance we can move her?"

"She can't be jostled right now," Lissa said. "Can you guarantee you'll move her without jostling her?"

"No."

"Then she stays."

"Okay, but the rest of them have to go," Clint said, "and so do you."

"No, if Katrina stays, I stay," Lissa said. "You can put the others somewhere else and Marietta will go with them."

Clint opened his mouth to argue but Lissa cut him off and said, "You'll be wasting your time and breath if you argue, Clint."

Clint looked at Deputy Boone, who asked, "Where are we puttin' them?"

"Somewhere close," Clint said. "Somewhere they all fit, and where they can be made comfortable."

"Hotel across the street," Boone said. "The rooms are expensive, but I'll talk to the sheriff. Can we do this in the mornin'?"

"No, tonight, under the cover of darkness," Clint said.

"All right," Boone said. "I'll go talk to Sheriff Brown and we'll arrange it. Can we bring back some help?"

"If you can trust them."

"We'll see," Boone said. "Ma'am, I'll be back."

"Thank you, Deputy Boone," Lissa said, "for everything."

"I haven't really done anythin' yet, ma'am."

"You've been here all this time with us, and Marietta and I appreciate it."

Boone actually blushed, stammered, and left.

"I better tell Marietta," Lissa said. "We can start getting the patients ready."

"Can I help?"

"Not 'til it's time to move them." She started for the other room, then stopped and turned. "You really think they'll come here?"

"This is where I'll be, so they'll come here," he said. "Also, if I'm right and Lillian Graham is behind this, they'll probably be looking to kill both you and Marietta as well."

"Oh," she said.

"Change your mind about staying?"

"No," she said. "The child will need me. But I'll get the rest of them ready to go."

THIRTY-NINE

It took over an hour, but Sheriff Brown, Deputy Boone, and Clint managed to move the patients to a hotel not across the street, but just down the street from the doctor's office. They were able to use the back doors of both buildings so that, from the street, everything seemed quiet.

"That the last one?" the sheriff asked.

"Yes," Clint said.

"What about the doctor?"

"She's staying because of the little girl with the injured leg."

"Does she know what she's in for?"

"I told her," Clint said, "and she's staying."

"You want Boone back, right?" Brown asked.

"If he'll come," Clint said. "If you'll let him."

"He'll have to take off his badge," Brown said.

"Why?"

"Because my office can't have anything to do with this," Brown said. "You're setting this up to be a massacre."

"I'm not looking to massacre anybody," Clint said.

"Well, they're gonna massacre you," Brown said, "and that lady doctor."

"They're going to try."

"Well," Brown said, "you're on your own, Adams, unless Boone wants to quit and help you."

"You're serious, aren't you?"

"I got the word from the mayor," Brown said. "If I want to keep my job, I keep my nose out of it."

"And arrest whoever's left, right?" Clint asked. "Maybe charge them with Graham's murder?"

"I'm just doin' my job, Adams," Brown said.

"You tell Boone I'll understand if he doesn't come back," Clint said.

"I'll tell him."

The sheriff left the way he came in, the back door.

When he was gone, Lissa came in.

"Was he serious?" she asked. "He's not going to help you?"

"He was serious."

"What kind of lawman is he?"

"The kind who wants to stay alive."

"What about Deputy Boone?" she asked. "He'll come and help you, won't he?"

"That'll be up to him," Clint said. "If I had to guess, I'd say no."

Clint walked over to Dr. Graham's desk and sat behind it. He had brought with him his rifle and his saddlebags. In the saddlebags he had shells for his modified Colt, the rifle, and the Colt New Line he'd given to Lissa.

"I'll make some coffee," she said.

"Don't you have to watch the girl?"

"She's asleep," she said. "She'll probably sleep through the night."

"Then you could have left with the others," he said as she prepared the coffee.

"I said she'll *probably* sleep through the night," Lissa said. "If not, I have to be here."

"I understand."

He put his rifle and pistol on top of the desk.

"What are you going to do?"

"I'm going to clean my weapons and make sure they're in proper working order," Clint said. "The last thing I want to do is go into a gunfight with guns that won't fire."

"Do you, uh, want this one?" She took the New Line from her pocket.

"Yes," he said. "I'll clean that one first."

She took it to the desk and set it down among the others.

"There's going to be lots of killing tomorrow, isn't there?"

"There's going to be shooting," Clint said. "How much killing gets done will be up to them."

"And this is all because of some silly woman who wanted her husband dead?"

"Apparently."

"Why didn't she just leave him?"

"Because then she wouldn't get his money, and the house, and his practice."

"What will she do with his practice?" Lissa asked.

"I have no idea," he said. "Could she sell it to another doctor?"

"I suppose so," Lissa said. "Although that would be like . . . buying his patients, wouldn't it?"

"I suppose."

He started cleaning the New Line. She went to check on the girl. By the time she came back, the gun was clean, and the coffee was ready.

"This hasn't gone the way you planned, has it?" she asked.

"I don't know," he said. "Rufus or Franco might just come tomorrow to talk, or maybe to call me out into the street."

"You wouldn't go, would you?"

"Be safer for you if this took place on the street," Clint said.

"What about you?"

"Might be safer for me, too."

"How so?"

"Well, out on the street I wouldn't have to worry about you and that little girl in there."

"Do you want to see her?" she asked.

"No."

She frowned.

"Why not? She's adorable."

"I'm sure she is, but it would put me in the wrong frame of mind," he said. "I'm just going to sit here, drink coffee, clean my guns, and imagine how this should go."

"What if nobody comes tomorrow?"

"That," he said, "would throw me off, and then I wouldn't know what to expect."

FORTY

"Did you hear?" Rufus asked Franco the next morning.

"You mean that Adams was lookin' for me? I heard it from Auntie."

They were at the saloon on the dock, where they were to meet the other men.

"Maybe we should wait," Rufus said.

"Wait for what?"

"Another time," Rufus said. "If we go to that office, Adams is going to be waiting for us."

"It does not matter," Franco said.

"He'll have the deputy with him."

"You and the others can take care of the deputy," Franco said. "I will take care of Clint Adams."

"He's all yours," Rufus said.

Franco poked Rufus in the chest with his forefinger.

"You just make sure you take care of the nurse," Franco said. "I have never been in jail because I never leave witnesses."

"I'll take care of her."

"You got money for the men?"

"Yeah," Rufus said, putting his hand in his pocket. "I got it from her this morning."

Franco eyed Rufus and said, "After you fucked her, eh?"

Yeah, Rufus thought, after he gave it to her good. He thought that, when it came time to kill her, he'd do it during sex. It was something he'd never done before.

"Give it to me," Franco said.

Rufus took the money out and handed it to the Mexican.

"American money," he said.

"That's what she had," Rufus said.

"The men will take it," Franco said.

"How much are we payin' them?"

"Fifty dollars each."

"There's a lot more than that there," Rufus said.

Franco smiled for the first time.

"I know," he said. "More for you and me." He put the money in his pocket. "You have a gun?"

"I have one," Rufus said. "On my horse."

"Well, strap it on, Rufus," Franco said. "It's time to go and earn all that money."

"Earn it?" Rufus asked, shaking his head. "What do you think I been doin' all these weeks sleepin' with that ugly woman?"

FORTY-ONE

Clint looked out the window at the street below.

"They know," he said.

"What?" Lissa asked.

"Come here."

She came over to stand next to him.

"What do you see?"

She stared at the street for a few moments, then said, "Nobody."

"That's right," he said.

"It's early."

"But not too early for people to be on the street. They know," Clint said. "They know something's going to happen today, and now so do we." He stepped away from the window, pulled her along. "From now on, don't go near the window."

"All right."

"You got that gun I gave you?"

She patted her pocket.

"I'm going to check the door," he said. "I want to make sure it's locked."

He went down the back way. The first floor of the building was empty. That was where Dr. Graham had been planning to put his hospital. The back door was locked, but the lock wasn't very good. In fact, the door wasn't very good. If he'd had a hammer and nails, he could have nailed it shut.

They had two ways to come up—front stairs and back stairs—but both stairways were narrow. They'd be really vulnerable on either of them.

So locking the doors was not a problem.

They weren't going to come up.

They were going to try to make him come down.

When Clint went back upstairs, Lissa asked, "Does it give you satisfaction?"

"What?"

"Knowing that you're right?"

"I don't know yet that I'm right," he said, "but I'd rather do this sooner than later. It's the waiting that gets to you."

"You?" she asked, smiling. "I'll bet nothing gets to you."

"Oh, there are things that get to me."

"Really? Like what?"

She was standing with her back to the window, backlit by the sun. Her hair seemed to glow. She was wearing a white doctor's coat, and under it a simple dress.

"You."

"What?"

"You get to me," he said, moving toward her.

"Clint."

He grabbed her by the shoulders, pulled her to him, and kissed her. The kiss went on for a long time. At first she was resistant, but gradually she melted into it and kissed him back. He slid his hand between them, undid her coat, and slid it off her, letting it drop to the floor. Next he pulled the dress down from her shoulders, so that her small breasts were exposed.

"Wait—" she said against his mouth.

He turned her, walked her backward until he had her pinned to the wall. He kissed her neck, her shoulders, and then her breasts. Her breath started to come in hard gasps. He slid his right hand down beneath her dress, into her underwear. He touched her, found her wet. She gasped again against his mouth. He took a nipple into his mouth, worried it, started to press a finger inside her.

"Wait," she said abruptly, "stop."

She wrestled herself free from him, backing away. Her breasts were exposed, the nipples hard, her chest heaving.

"Not here," she said to him, "and not now."

"When?"

"Later."

"What if there isn't a later?"

From the other room they both heard the little girl.

"God," she said, covering herself with her dress. She picked up her coat from the floor and hurried into the next room.

He walked to the window, put his hand to his mouth. He could smell her, taste her.

"Later," he said.

*   *   *

Franco looked up, saw Clint Adams standing in the window. Rufus was with him, in a doorway across the street. The others were down the street, waiting for the signal.

"Are we goin' up?" Rufus asked.

"No," Franco said, "he is going to come down."

"How are we gonna make him come down?"

"We don't have to make him," Franco said. "He wants to come down. Look at him."

Rufus looked up at Clint, still in the window.

"See him?" Franco said. "He wants to."

When Lissa came back into the room, he didn't turn. He knew she would be dressed again, buttoned up.

"I'm sorry," he said.

"Don't be," she said. "I've wanted you from the beginning. When this is over, we can be together, and then you can leave."

He saw movement across the street, saw the two men step out of the doorway.

"Clint?"

"You keep that gun handy," he told her.

"What?"

He turned and looked at her.

"Keep it handy," he said.

"You're not going down."

"I am."

"But—"

"You shoot anybody who comes through that door," he said, pointing to the front, and then he went down the back.

FORTY-TWO

Rufus looked down the street and signaled the other men to advance. When they reached Franco and Rufus, the Mexican said, "He's not in the window anymore. He is comin' down." He looked at the men. "You three watch the front door. He might decide to come out another way, but—"

"Franco," Rufus said, cutting him off. He looked at Franco, who jerked his head toward the street.

All the men looked in that direction and saw Clint Adams standing in the street.

Clint made his way to the alley that ran alongside the building, and walked out to the street. He saw Franco and Rufus—recognizable because of his size—being joined by four other men. So six, he thought, unless there's somebody on the roof. He looked up and didn't see anybody.

He stepped out into the street, immediately noticed by the six men.

"Which one is Franco?"

The Mexican standing next to Rufus stepped out.

"I am Franco."

"And I suppose the big fella next to you is Rufus?"

"That's right," Rufus said.

"You have been lookin' for me," Franco said. "Well, I am here."

"With a bunch of your friends, I see."

Franco nodded.

"I have many friends."

"I can see that."

"What is on your mind, my friend?"

"What's on my mind is avoiding bloodshed."

Franco shook his head.

"I am afraid that can't be," Franco said. "First I will kill you, then the lady doctor. She is upstairs?"

"No," Clint lied. "They're all gone."

"I will see for myself after I have killed you," Franco said. "Rufus, he will take care of the nurse."

"Sounds like you got it all planned out."

"I have." He gave a hand signal and the other five men fanned out, more than an arm's length between each of them. They all wore guns, but the only one who looked comfortable wearing one was Franco. Clint was going to have to key on him.

At that moment there was a flash of white in the window. Clint had told Lissa to stay out of sight, but she couldn't resist watching.

"Ah, there is the good doctor," Franco said, looking up. "I have heard she is quite beautiful. I will enjoy her before I kill her."

"And you're going to kill her just for money?" Clint said.

Franco shrugged.

"Why do I kill anyone?" he asked. "I do not enjoy it, but I am good at it."

"Well, I can say the same," Clint said. "What about your other men? Are they willing to risk—"

"There is no point in talking about them," Franco said, cutting him off. "They cannot understand English."

"So we're going to do this," Clint said, "on the whim of some silly woman."

"A silly, ugly, gringa woman," Franco said, "but sí, we are going to do this. After all, you are the Gunsmith. How could I not do this?"

Well, Clint thought, as reasons go, that one made a lot more sense.

Looking down from the window, Lissa Sugarman wanted to close her eyes or look away, but she could not. She watched the six men fan out, and didn't know how Clint expected to survive.

Rufus tried to move farther away from Franco. He was not a good hand with a gun, and hoped his size wouldn't make him a good target for the Gunsmith. Clint Adams would probably concentrate on Franco first, but after that, Rufus was concerned he'd be next. Shit, all he'd ever wanted was some sex and some money. How had he gotten here?

To Franco, Clint Adams looked calm—but then Franco himself was very calm inside. Men like him and the Gunsmith had been through this many times. But only one of them would go through it again.

Out of the corner of his eye, Clint saw Jim Boone and his shotgun move onto the boardwalk. There was no flash of silver on his chest.

"Your call," he said to Franco.

Franco nodded, but before the nod was complete, his hand went for his gun. This was the signal for the others to draw as well.

Clint drew his gun and fired before anyone else. Soon after, he heard the boom of the shotgun. His first shot took Franco in the chest, drove him back a few feet. The shotgun blast shredded Rufus Holmes before the big man knew what had hit him.

The four hired men did not see what had happened to Franco. They were still raising their weapons when Clint turned his attention to them. He fired twice, drowned out by a second shotgun blast. Two men were thrown off their feet, while the other two simply crumpled to the ground.

And suddenly, it was quiet.

People started to come out of the buildings.

Clint walked up to the bodies, was joined there by the shotgun-wielding Boone.

"Glad to see you," Clint said. "Hope this doesn't cost you your job."

"What the hell," Boone said. "Kyle's been kind of a disappointment to me since he took over the job."

Clint replaced his spent shells with live ones and holstered his gun. Boone did the same with his shotgun.

"Any more expected?" Boone asked.

"I don't think so," Clint said. "This was Franco's show."

"Hired by who?" Boone asked.

"Probably Rufus, acting for Mrs. Graham. Any chance we can get the sheriff to arrest her?"

"I doubt it," Boone said. "She's the widow of a prominent citizen. Don't think the mayor would approve."

"We'll have to make sure she doesn't send anyone after Dr. Sugarman again," Clint said.

"Seems to me you already got most everybody out of there," Boone said. "Once you move the girl and the doctor, Mrs. Graham gets her building back."

"That's true," Clint said. "But we still don't know who killed Dr. Graham."

"Yeah, we do," the deputy said. "The sheriff made an arrest last night."

"What? Who?"

"Manolo Gonzales," Boone said.

"Marietta's husband?"

"Not her husband, really, but yeah, he's the one. He was jealous, apparently."

"Of the doctor?"

Boone shrugged.

"That's why I don't have a woman, I guess. I don't understand it. I don't understand them, or the things men do for them."

Clint looked at him.

"You here because of me, or the doctor?" Clint asked.

They both looked up at the window, where Lissa was still standing, a relieved look on her face.

"Do you care?" Boone asked.

"No," Clint said, "I appreciate your help."

"What're your plans?" Boone asked.

"Just want to make sure Lillian Graham doesn't have any reason to go after Dr. Sugarman again," Clint said. "Then I'll be on my way."

"Well, I could stay around until the little girl is ready to be moved," Boone said. "Then we move her and the doctor, and that's it."

"The sheriff hasn't been much help, but maybe he could let the widow know what happened to Rufus and Franco. And tell her we know she was behind it."

"Seems to me she don't have no reason to stay in Veracruz after that," Boone said. "She can take her husband's money and be on her way."

Clint looked up again at Lissa, the taste and smell of her immediately coming to mind.

"I just have one or two more things to do," he said, "and I'll be on my way as well."

Watch for

THE BISBEE MASSACRE

340th novel in the exciting GUNSMITH series
from Jove

Coming in April!

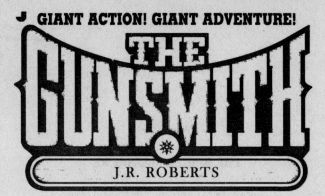

GIANT ACTION! GIANT ADVENTURE!

THE GUNSMITH

J.R. ROBERTS